# Christmas on Maplewood Mountain

## by
## Elizabeth Bromke

First Edition- October 2018

Published by:
Sarah Bromke
White Mountains, Arizona

For Little E.

# Chapter 1

Mary Delaney sat on the stool behind her reception desk and stared out the front window of the Lodge. It was already early December, but this was the first, real snow of the season. Leftover oak leaves peeked out from a blanket of snow, their dusty champagne hue glowing against the white.

*This was sudden,* Mary thought to herself as she recalled that it was still in the upper-fifties just the day before.

Lapping flames and glowing embers in the fireplace had only been for show up until that morning. Although, there hadn't been many people *to* show at good old Wood Smoke Lodge. In fact, it had been ten years since Wood Smoke Lodge was fully booked.

Still, Mary pressed on. She had just finished balancing her modest checkbook, so she stood up from her stool and stretched for a moment, before striding into the great room and up to the flagstone hearth.

There, she grabbed her worn, canvas tote and then went out to the back deck, where she filled the tote with five or so logs. She lugged the cleanly-chopped firewood back to the over-sized stone fireplace. Despite having the worst tourist season yet, Mary enjoyed following the routines she had established over the years. Tending the fire was maybe her favorite.

Every year by the first of November, Mary's dad and two brothers, Robert and Alan, would be finished cutting down and chopping up nearly a dozen cords of wood: enough to fill five or six truckloads and a season's worth of warmth for all four of the properties- one for her parents' farmhouse, one each for Robert's and Alan's houses, and one for Mary's home and business- Wood Smoke Lodge.

Mary couldn't decide if she wanted a husband to be out there working alongside the men in her family- cutting and hauling wood in their spare time. But of one thing she was certain: she was tired of relying on

1

her parents and brothers for her livelihood. None of her other three sisters did.

Anna, Mary's older sister by a mere ten months, was considered the black sheep by her parents. Even in the face of her impressive professional success in the tech sector, Margaret and Warren Delaney expected a more traditional life of their children: the boys were to work the family farm. The girls were to become homemakers.

Anna was a lost cause.

The second oldest, Roberta, was also questionable. Roberta, like Anna, was a little wild. But, the Delaneys reasoned, at least Roberta didn't chase a career and fame as Anna seemed to. And while Anna was open about her flagrant affairs, Roberta was private.

Warren and Margaret saw that Mary might have a chance of taking after her oldest sister, Erica, who had settled down early and enjoyed being a wife and mother more than was natural.

A shrill ring burst from the front desk just as Mary stacked the second log on the grate. She pushed off the hearth and trotted back to the little reception area.

"Hello?" Mary chirped into the receiver, "Wood Smoke Lodge, this is Mary?"

"Where have you been? I must have sent you forty texts." It was Anna, of course. Only Anna and their mother ever seemed to call.

Mary sighed in disappointment, worrying herself further over the distinct lack of bookings this winter.

"Anna, you know I am not glued to my phone like you. Why do you even bother?" It was true, Mary was regrettably low-tech. In fact, Anna would regularly blame Mary's ineffective business practices on her refusal to upgrade to the twenty-first century. Mary didn't totally disagree. But life on Maplewood Mountain sort of limited her opportunities. Internet barely existed up there.

"Well, if you had read my texts, then you wouldn't be huffing into the phone. I, as usual, have an incredible idea," Anna's singsong voice further irritated Mary.

"Is this like your 'Move to the city and we can be roommates' idea? Or more along the lines of 'Move to Europe and let the Lodge fall into foreclosure as a business decision' idea?" Mary regularly had to decline Anna's wild notions of how she might find success or happiness.

"Better. Hear me out. So, FantasyCoin is doing exceptionally well at the moment, as you know," Anna started.

"I did not, but go on." Mary could not figure out the cryptocurrency madness of which her sister was a part. She was confused even by the stock market, so digital money meant little to her.

"Well, it is. Kurt is on fire," Anna began to continue.

"Wait, Kurt? As in, the boring boss who you claim is successful only because of family money?"

"Yeah, whatever. Boring. Spoiled. Whatever. He *is* successful, however. And, part of that success comes from FantasyCoin. Cut him some slack," Anna returned.

"Okay, go on."

"So, we, Kurt included, are on fire with the product and investors. Now that football season is well underway, we've been able to see that Fantasy Football players have been desperate for exactly what we are creating and selling. We have officially moved beyond getting the average consumer to download the app; now we have big Fantasy Football Leagues dying to invest."

Mary was utterly confused. First cryptocurrency, now Fantasy Football. She had no idea how she was related to Anna, who was working for a company that combined these two foreign concepts.

The dead air gave way to Anna's forced patience with her sister.

"Mary, Stay with me. Anyways, so Kurt read that all these tech companies out of Silicon Valley and Downtown Phoenix are planning quarterly retreats as a reward and incentive for their employees. You know: a chance to connect and blow off steam and do obnoxious ice-breakers. Well, Kurt had me book our team a spot in one of the local company retreats in Downtown Phoenix, but yesterday we got a call saying that it was canceled. So, now, we are desperate to find a spot on short notice. This brings me to my point."

Mary was still lost. She felt a shiver course through her as she craned her neck to check on the fireplace. Dry wood was waiting for her. "I have a million things to do today. What, exactly, *is* your point?" Only a slight exaggeration. Getting the fire started always seemed to take the better part of an hour.

"Wood Smoke Retreat," Anna chimed in with crisp satisfaction. "We are going to turn the Lodge into a *Retreat*."

# Chapter 2

Kurt Cutler took his lunch break at 10:30am every day. He knew his employees liked to enjoy their own lunch without their boss eavesdropping on their midday chatter. So, he would tuck away into the break room an hour earlier. There, he would unwrap his brown bag lunch methodically and scan the news on his phone. Kurt appreciated routine, especially when it came to work.

He started with a crisp apple and then moved quickly onto his turkey and lettuce on wheat. He skipped through the financial pages and skimmed over pop culture as he chomped away.

Finally, he clicked off his phone and popped the last bite into his mouth, his strong jaw crunching through the sandwich neatly. He drew his soda to his lips, the tin can dwarfed in his brawny hand. He only drank soda once or twice a month, when he really needed a pick-me-up.

The day before, he'd learned that the company retreat he had planned was canceled. The downtown Phoenix hotel, which hosted corporate retreats or conferences nearly every weekend, had contacted him to express their regret at the cancellation of FantasyCoin's First Annual Company Retreat. When Kurt asked for an explanation, the hotel manager indicated there had been an emergency with the retreat host. They weren't sure if there would be an opportunity to reschedule. FantasyCoin did receive a full refund, but Kurt was crushed.

He had been looking forward to the weekend after next ever since they had booked back in September. Sales were soaring: between new investors and product downloads, it was looking like FantasyCoin was about to surpass every other cryptocurrency in the rankings, with the exception of Bitcoin. With that kind of momentum, Kurt wanted to make sure he was running his business like he knew what he was doing.

Kurt had founded FantasyCoin on the heels of making good money in his father's company, a traditional investment group that served wealthy Phoenix clientele.

5

At the time, Kurt's divorce had finally drawn to a close, and he had lost any interest in pursuing the life he thought he wanted. Brittany, his ex, wasn't a bad person. But after ten years of ups and downs, Kurt realized that he was no longer willing to settle for a woman who put her career (and other men) ahead of her own husband and their future together. Kurt took some solace in the fact that Brittany had scoffed at his desire to start a family.

Before leaving Cutler Investments, Kurt had been playing with Bitcoin and other new cryptocurrencies, but it was in his Fantasy Football teams that he saw a need. His team lacked an unbiased, automated commissioner. Kurt had friends who could build an app that would fix this, but he wanted to monetize it well enough to ensure he would never have to work for his father again. And so, FantasyCoin was born.

Kurt swallowed down the last of the soda and crushed the can in his palm. He felt himself growing even tenser. His disappointment over the retreat cancellation felt a little out of proportion. But slogging through the day in another white-walled office, no matter how wildly successful FantasyCoin was becoming, had begun to make him feel empty.

He sighed, leaned back, and stared out the small break room window. His gaze was met with blue skies peeking out between a series of sterile, lifeless skyscrapers. *It might be December*, he thought, *but at FantasyCoin, it didn't feel like Christmas.*

# Chapter 3

Mary returned to her perch behind her desk, deciding to focus her attention on digging around under the desktop for the furniture oil and rag. Once she found the bottle, with its rag draped over the top like a wet wig, she set about rubbing the oil into the wood grain.

"I have no idea what you're talking about. Wood Smoke Retreat?" Mary replied, her confusion turning to irritation as she worked the rag into the corner behind the cash register.

Anna cleared her throat dramatically. "Wood Smoke Lodge... my dear, sweet sister's wilting little inn is going to offer a promo! Company retreats!" Anna all but cheered into the phone.

"What? What do you mean a *promo*?"

"We are going to give the good ol' Lodge a little shock to the system. I am officially resurrecting that sleepy old place into the premier tourist attraction of Maplewood Mountain."

"Come on, Anna, don't be ridiculous. I have no idea how that could even work. Have you forgotten that tourism has slowed down drastically in the last decade? Not happening," Mary was used to being let down by disappointing offers of turning her life around in some magical way. Especially from Anna.

"Okay, then I'll try a different approach. Mary, as your older sister, I'm demanding that you rebrand. My proposal is for you to offer weekend getaway packages to couples, or companies, or even singles. You can take whatever angle you'd like. I don't care. But, I strongly encourage you to think of an angle as soon as possible, because without it- this idea doesn't work." Anna finished her lecture and sat quietly on the other end of the line.

Mary took a moment herself. What did she have to lose? She was already losing. Every month. The Lodge had basically been her own home and little more. Sure, there was a steady trickle of curious out-of-towners who would book with her about once a week. But, the lodge was a long ways from thriving.

When Mary had bought it, ten years before, the realtor told her that it was the most popular ski lodge on the mountain. That wasn't saying much since Maplewood was such a tiny town. Still, Mary found herself curious about what the lodge would be like if it were booked solid with ski bunny types and diehard snowboarders. She would love to host families from the valley who wanted to get out of the summer heat. She could even take big-city tech executives, she figured.

Generally, Mary enjoyed a quiet, peaceful lifestyle. But the loneliness could be suffocating. Dealing with the pressure from her parents to meet some Maplewood good ol' boy was too much to handle any longer. And besides, Mary wanted true love. Not convenience.

Mary decided her sister might actually have a good idea.

"Whatever it takes," she replied at last.

"You're game? Oh my gosh!" Anna screamed into the phone. "Awesome! Okay, wow, so here is the next step. I'm going to pitch this to Kurt. Maplewood is only a four-hour drive. We'll have the chance to get out of the bustle of the big city. It'll be beautiful up there this time of year. It's the perfect locale for what he has in mind. You just work on the theme of your new 'Retreat Weekend Promo,' okay?" Anna was all but gushing.

"Wait, what do you mean theme? Why can't it just be a getaway? Like a vacation? The employees can just come and relax," Mary suggested.

"No, no, no. These things always have an angle. You know, like Hawaiian Luau or Under the Sea."

"Those sound like prom themes, not business retreats, Ann," Mary laughed.

"Whatever. Okay, maybe a better example is this one conference I went to last summer. The focus was communication in the digital age- how to best make use of social media," Anna continued.

A familiar disappointment crawled through Mary's stomach as she realized that there was something wrong with this after all.

"Ehh, that's not at all up my alley. I would do better with the prom themes," Mary whined.

"No, no. Don't get overwhelmed. We'll keep it simple. How about-," Anna paused, thoughtfully. "How about *Christmas in the Pines? A Wood Smoke Lodge Retreat?*"

The line went silent for what felt like an eternity.

"I love it," Mary said, quietly.

# Chapter 4

"Hey, boss. No rush, but when you're back from lunch, I'd love a moment of your time." Anna didn't wait for an answer, but instead ducked back out of the break room and into the office, letting the door whoosh closed.

Kurt wiped the few crumbs on the table into his hand and tossed them into his paper bag, which he dropped into the receptacle.

He had hired Anna because of how dynamic she was. But she always seemed to be on-the-go, and it frequently made him uneasy. He had come to expect daily strikes from her. Sometimes they were small things, like when the building maintenance staff forgot to restock the women's bathroom. Sometimes they were big things, like when she had figured a way to save a couple thousand dollars in operating costs. Still, Kurt could never tell when she had a small concern or a big idea. Anna was unpredictable that way.

Kurt loosened his necktie an inch, and left the break room, heading for the coffee bar. He didn't care much for the tech world trends in office feng shui, but his vice president, Anna Delaney, definitely did. He appreciated the convenience an open-air office afforded, but he especially loved always being near the water cooler, where he refilled his aluminum tumbler at least three times a day.

"Kurt, I wanted to pick your brain a little further on the company retreat idea," Anna caught him just as he bent over for his second refill. Where she had scurried to and from since she barged into the break room was a mystery to him.

"Oh right, I'm a little stressed about it. Did anything else turn up?" Kurt asked, hoping they would find a replacement retreat soon. He hadn't taken a trip since just before the divorce, over a year ago. Kurt wasn't much for travel, but he needed an escape. And while he was all-in on FantasyCoin, and being in the heart of football season with the new project was exciting, the stress could be crippling.

Kurt's parents didn't help the matter. Wealth and magazine covers weren't enough for Kurt Cutler Senior or his wife, Diane. Cryptocurrency and blockchain-based projects like Bitcoin did not impress the traditional finance magnate. The Cutlers thought that decentralizing money by digitizing it was nothing short of a scam. And who truly had use for a decentralized public ledger outside of tech enthusiasts? So the Cutlers said, anyway.

Anna busied herself with making a fresh cup of espresso as she replied, evenly, "Well, I think I may have the perfect solution." She stirred in a packet of raw sugar.

"Oh?" Kurt raised his eyebrows.

"It's something that would save us a little bit of money. After all, while I know our books are looking great, it wouldn't hurt to be conservative as we move into the holiday shopping season." Anna's voice was neutral, but Kurt could feel a catch coming.

"Go on," he said as he set down his water and adjusted his waistband unnecessarily, a nervous habit. Anna's eyes momentarily caught at his trim midsection. They darted back up, awkwardly.

"Okay, so, I know this may sound like a conflict of interest- but I assure you I've thought it through," Anna continued. "My sister runs a very rustic lodge in the mountains north of the city. Have you ever been to Maplewood?"

"No, but my family does have a place in the White Mountains," he replied, flatly. The White Mountains were a different range farther north. Kurt didn't elaborate but instead waited for her to make her case.

"Okay, sure. Well, Maplewood is this sleepy little mountain town. Actually, it's where I grew up. My family has a farm there, and my sister owns a bed-and-breakfast type, um, retreat in town. Wood Smoke Retreat," Anna glanced to the right nervously as she paused.

"Oh, really? Does she host company retreats regularly?" Kurt was immediately, and surprisingly, interested.

"Yes. It's very... rural and downhome. No frills. Get back in touch with nature, mountain-life stuff. It could be perfect!" Her excitement gave way.

"Does she have corporate experience? How does she run her program? Does she have an opening for two weeks out? That's certainly our biggest obstacle," he started to trail off.

"She has been running the lodge for ten years, and I'm not really sure what you mean by program. And, yes. I am certain there will be an opening for our preferred date, but I can double check," Anna seemed to regain her voice, ending on a confident note.

Kurt furrowed his brow, keeping his arms taut across his chest. "Get me a website, and I'll take a look," he said finally, retrieving his water from the table and heading back to his desk. Before sitting down, he returned his gaze to Anna, who was left at the coffee bar, mouth slightly agape. "Sounds promising, Anna," he nodded at her.

# Chapter 5

Mary spent the rest of the day in cleaning mode. She finished polishing the reception area then went to grab the dustpan and brush to clear out the fireplace before starting up the fire. She felt a renewed energy course through her veins.

Once one of the logs began to smolder, she closed the chain grate and clapped off the soot from her lap. Standing, she turned and took in the great room. The high ceilings were draped in spider webs. A good cleaning was long overdue.

When Mary bought the property, she whipped it into shape. With nothing more than a little elbow grease, the old parts came back to life so much so that it didn't need much in the way of renovations.

With a small loan from her parents, Mary invested in new furniture for the great room and guest rooms. Wood grain this, and studded leather that. She ended up being able to make do with the appliances and dining table that the former owners had left behind. The heavy cast iron woodstove was too beautiful to replace. Same went for the charming and expansive farm table and matching benches.

Using her old skeleton key, Mary opened the door to each guest room. The only guests who had booked for the week had checked out early that morning. She decided the place could do for a little airing out. Deep cleaning felt in order.

As she was stripping the bed, it occurred to Mary that she had no idea how she had been spending her time lately. She had done little outside of reading, some light baking with the apples from her parents' tree, and walking aimlessly around the lodge.

How depressing. Maybe Anna had a good point. Mary smiled to herself, sadly. Maybe Mary really did need a kick in the pants.

By five o'clock in the evening, the whole of the lodge was as oiled and scrubbed as it could be. Mary went to the two big wooden doors that made for the entrance and flung them open, in defiance of the heavy snowfall. She breathed in the cool, smoky air and took a good look out, admiring the aspen-lined drive. The property sat only fifty yards or so from Maplewood's main street, but it felt private enough, especially with the thick forest that filled the acreage.

Leaving the doors yawning open, Mary walked back to the kitchen and pulled the kettle from atop the fridge. She added a couple mugs' worth of milk and set it to boil on the old cast iron stove. Then, she rummaged in the small pantry for her cocoa powder. It wasn't too far behind the dry oatmeal. After grabbing her one-and-only Christmas mug, Mary shoveled a hearty helping of powder into it. She poured in the milk and stirred her mug absent-mindedly as she walked out the open doors and plodded down the stairs of the front deck.

Several careful sips later, Mary arrived at the storage shed on the side of the lodge. She pushed back her hood and brushed accumulated snow off her shoulders.

Then, cautiously, Mary popped open the weathered lock, stepped inside, and eyed the Christmas decorations bins. They were lodged down beneath the Halloween and Thanksgiving boxes. Disappointed in herself for putting off the holiday cheer until after the first of December, she resolved to never again to waste a Black Friday stalking the local antique shops aimlessly.

Setting her mug on the ground, she heaved out the bins and popped the lids. Off in the distance, she heard a couple cars and trucks rumbling slowly up the mountain and past the property. She didn't expect anyone to stop, but she couldn't help but glance up with the purr of each oncoming engine.

With each passing vehicle that didn't stop, her heart grew heavier. Once the vehicles passed by, she tugged the three bins out of the shed. Just as she was about to grab her mug and close the door, she flipped back around.

The Christmas tree.

Now, where was that? It was a pre-lit faux tree that cost as much as Mary was making in a week. She didn't see its silhouette among the clutter of the shed, but there was nowhere else it could be. She set her mug back down and clawed back into the shed, pulling up bins and shifting random tools and wooden boards. After a solid five minutes of searching the tiny shack, she gave up and hauled the bins to the front deck, snow crunching with every step.

As Mary stomped the snow off her boots on the doormat, she heard the trill of the reception desk phone. She swung the door open and raced in.

"Hello? Wood Smoke Lodge. Mary speaking." She whooshed into the receiver on the fifth ring.

"Yes, I'd like to reserve all seven of your rooms for the weekend after next, please?" It was Anna's teasing voice.

"Very funny. Don't get my hopes up," Mary sighed with disappointment.

"I'm not kidding, Mary. I think we are going to make this work."

"What are you talking about?"

"Kurt is interested in us booking with you. There is only one problem," Anna went on.

"Okay?"

"He wants to see a website, and he wants to know what the focus of your retreat is."

Mary slumped onto the barstool and combed her wavy locks to the side.

"I have no website. I have no angle. I would have no idea where to start on either of those, Ann." Her voice became more despondent as she realized that this wouldn't work, after all.

"Mary, these problems are solvable. I can throw together a website for you. But we need an angle. A theme. And a program, too."

"A retreat theme? Program? I have nothing to offer high-tech millionaires when it comes to business advice." Mary slid farther down until the left side of her face was resting on her arm on the wooden desktop.

"Well, luckily for you I think we just go with low key."

"Okay, well, relaxation is the leading reason anyone would come spend time at this place," Mary snorted. "At least until the slopes open next weekend."

"Hm, well, I figured that since it's December, we can capitalize on Christmas time. Magic of Christmas? All that?" Mary started to wonder if Anna was just going to take over completely. Maybe she should let her?

Anna continued. "Take advantage of the winter weather and holiday spirit, Mary! It can be a Christmas retreat. Hot chocolate, s'mores, trimming the tree... wait. Have you decorated yet? Is the lodge at all festive right this minute?"

"Um, well. I was *just* pulling the decorations. I haven't quite started, I wanted to focus on cleaning. And, um, I can't find the tree," Mary admitted.

"No, no, no. This could be a good thing. I mean, you have to set the vibe a little for us. But, why not let FantasyCoin employees do the decorating? It can be one of their retreat activities!"

"Activities?" Mary's head was spinning. "You mean like a Christmas camp for adults?" Life came to Mary's voice. This sounded like her kind of project.

"Yes!" Anna joined in her delight.

"I got it!" Mary was all but squealing. "A Corporate Christmas Retreat!"

Mary bolted up from the stool practically knocking it back into the key rack cabinet. Quickly righting the chair, she started giggling. Anna joined in.

"Yeah! Something like that. Now start thinking of how we can make this happen! I have to get back into the office."

"Thank you, Ann!"

"Oh, and Mary. I'll get going on the website later tonight. Don't worry about it. Just focus on getting the Lodge into tip-top shape. We got this."

Mary smiled to herself as she hung up the receiver. Mary didn't think she needed saving, but Anna was about to do just that.

# Chapter 6

"Rural Christmas?" Kurt read over Anna's right shoulder onto her computer. "Please tell me rural doesn't mean backwoods," Kurt pointed out, as he stared at the pine tree-trimmed homepage lighting up her computer screen. Kurt actually didn't care, though. Sure, he didn't want to be scammed into some hokey family scheme, but he trusted Anna. He was even warming to the idea of shutting his phone off and staring off into a campfire for a couple nights.

Maybe, instead of going high tech, it was time he went a little more low-tech. Still, Kurt wasn't sure if the others would enjoy it.

"I know it's nothing flashy. The website, I mean. But the Lodge really is beautiful. As beautiful as the setting. And, this will be a relaxing and invigorating experience with opportunities for team building. It's the perfect balance. Plus, who doesn't love Christmas?" Anna replied, triumphantly.

"Okay?" He prodded her on.

"Kurt, listen. Like I mentioned before, we need to be mindful of the expense account. And, secondly, I think there is a lot to be said for doing something with a spiritual or even nature-based aspect, as opposed to a sterile hotel ballroom conference." Her words came out like a rehearsed script.

He chuckled. "I generally agree, Anna. But I'm not sure the team would. They need to be plugged in. These people have a hard time going without their favorite mobile apps for more than five minutes. Wouldn't it be best to keep some degree of connection to the real world?" He was torn. He could see that being tucked away in the woods might be good for him, but he didn't want to rock the boat with the people who were the bread and butter of the company. "I don't see how we could sell this to the rest of the company."

"It's one weekend. I think we all need this. Finding ourselves. Learning about each other apart from who can code the fastest or who can

17

build the best social media platform." Anna met his gaze again, surefooted in her quest.

Uncrossing his arms, Kurt scratched his jawline and looked meaningfully into the space above Anna. "If you can convince the others, then I'm in, too." He clapped his hands together, loudly, and the rest of the office looked up, each pulling off his or her headphones and swiveling around to face Kurt and Anna.

There was Maci, who headed up social media for FantasyCoin. Jacen covered general marketing. Alex, Rory, and Kato managed coding and dabbled with the servers. Eddie was the everyman- handling general operations. They patiently watched Kurt, who finally cracked a smile.

"Okay, gang, let's talk company retreat. Anna thinks she has found a replacement retreat for the canceled one. I don't know if you guys are excited as I am, but, this thing is really important to me. It's my way of rewarding your hard work and validating our profession. Cryptocurrency can only go mainstream if quality coins continue to work for the users. I really believe in what we are doing with FantasyCoin, and I want us to continue on in our success." Kurt hesitated, wondering if he was sounding too preachy. When no one rolled their eyes, he finished his impromptu speech. "With that, I want your honest feedback on what Anna has to share." He repositioned himself at an angle against the wall and opened his arm in a gesture toward her. "Anna? Take it away."

# Chapter 7

Mary was feeling like her old self again, like the woman she was when she bought the lodge and had big dreams of becoming the Delaney family's first ever successful businesswoman. Of course, her sister ended up beating her out. But, Mary was always genuinely happy for Anna. And anyway, Mary ended up seeing a different future for herself. When Mary thought of success, she didn't envision fancy cars or loads of money. She pictured herself running the lodge alongside a true partner. Someone she was madly in love with. A man who would help her raise a family of their own.

But Mary knew the lodge's lack of success was not because of a missing man. It was because of something that was missing *in Mary*. Anna's idea for this retreat had brought this truth to the surface.

Today, however, Mary was feeling on top of the world. Like she could tackle this problem. Like there was a future for the lodge- man or no man.

After bringing the decorations inside to thaw out, Mary had set about making the guest beds.

She finished tucking the plaid flannel sheets and pulling up the thick wool blankets on the quaint little double bed in The Elk Room (each of the rooms was named for a woodland creature-- her own idea). After smoothing her hand across the wool, she walked to the doorway of the room and grabbed the old bronze door handle. Before closing it, she gazed into the room. She took in the hardwood floor and braided red rug that spread between the bed and the oak dresser. Her eyes drifted to the bedside clock. Not even digital. No alarm, either. No artwork or framed pictures hung in the room, but she had hung a small pair of elk antlers above the pine headboard. The pinewood walls added all the texture this room needed.

Mary just loved the way the lodge *felt*. She couldn't help but imagine a pair of lovebirds checking into the Elk room and falling onto the cozy bed, tired from a day of snowshoeing, but not too tired to lace fingers and talk the night away as they stared out through the frosted window at the falling snow.

She couldn't lose that *feeling*. What Mary was missing all this time wasn't money or notoriety. She was missing commitment. She needed to throw herself into something, for once in her life. Something more than buying the Lodge and letting it drift into nothingness.

She thought about the last time she had been on a date. It was with John Cook, who lived with his mom behind the old elementary school. He was a nice enough guy. He worked for the electric company and hunted and fished in his spare time.

Mary's parents loved him. Mary tolerated him. For their date, he took her to a rodeo in the next town over. Mary didn't mind the rodeo, but it wasn't really an interest of hers. Still, she sat through it as John cheered and whooped for the two events they'd watched.

As he drove her home, John asked if she had any vacancy in the Lodge. Naïvely, she thought he was inquiring about how business was going.

When she replied that yes, she had several available rooms, he squeezed her thigh and licked his lips. She felt like she was going to be sick and promptly demanded that he leave her at the corner drugstore on the way into Maplewood.

Her brother, Robert, picked her up half an hour later and took her home. He offered to stay the night there to make sure she was comfortable. But, she was fine.

Mary couldn't picture spending a night with someone like John. Not in the Elk Room. Not anywhere.

Giving the room one last nod of approval, she then shook the memory from her mind, smiled to herself, and closed the door on the room and the memory both. She withdrew her skeleton key from her pocket, locked the door, and stepped back. Closing her eyes for a minute to relish her newfound confidence, she turned left and headed down the hall to her own room - what she liked to refer to as the innkeeper's suite. A place she kept sacred to her heart.

# Chapter 8

Kurt was going over the server activity with Eddie when Anna returned from the lobby.

She brushed a strand of her reddish hair behind her ear and cleared her throat. Kurt stood, waiting to hear if Anna's sister had enough openings.

"We're in!" Anna beamed at the office as everyone waited for confirmation that they were, in fact, getting their snowy mountain getaway.

"Aww!" Maci clapped enthusiastically, "How adorable! I love it! Anna, did you know that my family went to Maplewood when I was little?" Maci picked up the chatter she had left off when Anna stepped out to call Mary.

"Great!" Anna replied with sincere enthusiasm, but she waited for more input as the others started to murmur to each other.

"Sounds good to me," Eddie offered a fist bump to Rory who then chimed in.

"What's the plan? Does she provide break-out sessions, or?" He asked.

"No, not really break-out sessions. In fact, it's going to be a little old-fashioned," Anna replied.

"That could be cool," Jace offered, stealing a peek at his half-pocketed phone. The others joined in on the buzz. Anna turned back to grin at Kurt, who was watching the rest of the group. He caught her eye, nodded, and winked.

"Glad it's a welcome decision," he said to no one in particular. "Do you have any other details for us, Anna?"

Anna's eyes darted back to the others.

"Right," she returned. "Really quickly, everyone. Let's talk specifics. First of all, it's much colder up there, of course. Pack your winter clothes. We'll be staying Friday and Saturday nights. Each team member will get his or her own room. All meals will be provided, including some light

21

snacks and beverages. And, it's going to be somewhat Christmas-themed," she started.

"Score!" Kato called out.

"Yay!" Maci acted like she was going to break out in happy tears.

"One more thing before I'm done. This is going to be a little new for us," she began as she focused her attention on the group in front of her, not looking back to see if Kurt was nodding his approval. "But, this event will be relatively tech-free. Phone-free. Computer-free. You can bring your phone for emergencies, but the reception will be limited," she stopped, searching the group for some reaction. She could hear Kurt behind her, shifting his weight. No one seemed to move for a minute. Then, Eddie, awkwardly, started a slow clap. Maci giggled. Alex joined in. Then Kato. Then Rory, until there was a full-blown applause.

Anna opened her stance, stepping back so that she could watch Kurt's response and that of the rest. Kurt met her eyes and broke into a wide smile, his hands moving to his hips.

"Excellent," he said, finally. As the applause died down and everyone began to chat excitedly, Jace spoke up.

"Quick question, Kurt. Or Anna," he started.

"Sure, what's up?" Kurt took back control.

"Who will oversee our day-to-day operations? Who will handle customer correspondence? We can't just go dead for an entire weekend. I mean, if we really are going to have limited cell service." His voice was steady and the question fair. But everyone quieted instantly, looking worriedly at Kurt then Anna.

Kurt pushed off the wall and crossed his arms in front of his chest. Smoothly, he responded, "That's an excellent question, and one I already considered back in September. Tech or no tech, I didn't want any of us working. So I reached out to a local temp agency. We are paying people to take over for us. It'll be a skeleton crew, but everything should operate as normal until we get back. This retreat is completely and utterly work-free."

The rest of the office fell back into a chorus of clapping and high-fiving. Anna walked up to Kurt.

"Thanks, Kurt. I had no idea. I'll use the company card to place the reservation and get an itinerary from my sister right away."

"Excellent. Nice work, Anna. This will be a great event." Anna nodded and began to turn back towards her desk. "Oh, Anna, one more thing."

"Yes?" She faced him again.

"I'd like to look further into this location and read up on your sister. Her name is Mary? Mary Delaney?"

"Um, yes. Mary Delaney. But, Kurt?" She looked up at him, waiting until he was focused to continue. "She's not online."

# Chapter 9

Mary decided to touch base with Anna. She was dying to know how her pitch went.

Once inside the knotty pine walls of her room, she rounded her own little double bed and untethered her cell phone from its charger. She wasn't totally out of touch; it was a smartphone and only a couple years old. But her data plan was limited and the reception even more so.

She noticed she had missed a call from her sister, Erica. She hadn't spoken to Erica in weeks, and even though she was anxious to get the scoop from Anna, she decided to make sure Erica was okay.

Erica answered just as Mary thought the phone was about to go to voicemail.

"Hello, Mare?" Erica panted breathlessly into the phone.

"Eri, hi!" Mary and Erica only ever called each other by their little pet names. "How are you? It's been forever!"

"I know, oh my gosh, give me a sec, sis. I just ran up the stairs to catch your call," Erica laughed into the phone and Mary joined her.

"Take your time, I'm so glad to hear your voice. It's been way too long."

After a few moments, Erica came back on the line. "Okay, whew! I'm recovered. I know it has! Mare, I have been very, very busy," Erica cooed suggestively and then giggled some more.

"What's that supposed to mean?" Mary was suspicious. Erica always acted a bit like a teen girl who was madly in love, no matter what it was she was talking about. Mary figured it had to do with the fact that Erica had never had a real job. She just didn't seem to grow up or age.

"You know just what it means!" Erica shouted back. "Mare, I'm pregnant!" This followed by a shrill squeal that Mary joined in on.

"Oh, Eri! I'm so, so happy for you! How far along are you?"

"Exactly eight weeks today. Jake didn't want to share the news until I was twelve weeks, but I told him fat chance. I have three sisters in my life, after all." Mary could hear the smile in Erica's voice and felt a twinge of envy. She forced herself to carry on in congratulating her sister before Erica had to get off the phone.

Moments later, Mary plodded down the expansive wooden staircase in her scuffed work boots and pulled up Anna's contact in her phone. Anna picked up on the first ring.

"Hey, give me a sec," she said, keeping her voice low into the phone. Mary waited without replying.

Finally, Anna returned.

"Okay, hi! Oh my gosh, great timing. I was about to text you. We just wrapped up a meeting on the retreat," Anna's voice was still low, which told Mary she must be in the restroom or perhaps the lobby of the office building.

"And? Is Kurt on board?" Mary asked, excitement filling her body.

"Yes," Anna hissed. "*Everyone* is on board, Mary- we have a green light!" she finished.

"Wow!" Mary couldn't contain herself. "Okay, I have less than two weeks to prep. What do I need to do? Other than decorate? Can you think of anything?" Mary asked, frantic.

"Yes, actually. Kurt asked for an itinerary. Can you email one over?"

"Sure. I'm about done with cleaning the rooms. I can take a break and run to the library, assuming they are open." She would need a computer. Growing up in Maplewood meant that no one ever knew what business or service would be open on what days or at what times. They called it "Mountain Time" for a reason. Mary didn't care if it wasn't open, today. She'd drive into the next town over to put something together if she needed to. Dancing a little jig in the middle of the lodge, she started for the kitchen to retrieve her keys to head to Maplewood Public Library.

"And," Anna interrupted Mary's glee. "The itinerary needs some activities. Even just one or two little ones."

"On it," Mary confirmed. Just as she was about to get off the phone, she remembered something. "Oh, Ann. Did Erica call you yet?"

"No, but I got a text from her. Baby number three, right? So wild," Anna scoffed. She was never an overly-sentimental type. They ended their call and Mary realized that it wasn't envy that she felt about Erica's news. Instead, she thought that the new baby was a good omen. A sign of hope.

# Chapter 10

A week of work had come and gone. More ten-hour days of reviewing website traffic, hosting conference calls with investors, and slogging through an ever-increasing backlog of emails. The weekend brought no reprieve since Kurt had to spend it prepping the temp agency to take over for the retreat weekend. But now it was Wednesday, and he really wanted to get packed. That way he could stay late at work on Thursday, if need be, and leave with the rest of the group on Friday, after lunch.

The weather had been nice in Phoenix. Late November into December the temperature rarely climbed past 75 or dipped below 50.

But Kurt was sick of it. Sick of a lot of things about the city, in fact. Sick of living on a concrete island. Sick of being stuck in rush-hour traffic. Sick of hipster boutiques and big box stores alike. Sick of chain restaurants, no matter how healthy or how diverse their menus. He needed a change. Even if the change was only a weekend vacation

When Anna pitched the mountains in his very own state, he could have kicked himself for not thinking of it.

He pulled his black duffle bag from the top shelf of his walk-in, shooting Anna a text simultaneously. He had forgotten to send the weekly newsletter email, and he knew she was probably still working.

He pulled an old college sweatshirt off a hanger then tossed a few more casual pieces into the bag.

After adding wool socks and a black beanie to the bag, he pulled his phone back out and brought up the weather app to see if he'd need his ski jacket. After seeing that Anna had responded with a "got it," he dismissed her messaged and typed *Maplewood, AZ* into the search bar, but no results matched. There happened to be four others- Minnesota, Missouri, Montana, and New Jersey. No Arizona.

How could Maplewood not even register on the app? Was it on a *map*, even? This concern reminded him of his earlier mission. He set his phone down on top of the bag and left his bedroom to head into the second room of the condo, what he originally thought would become a guest room for his mom or dad, or maybe an out-of-town friend. It turned out that he had no use for a guest room. His parents, after all, lived in Phoenix, too. And if they ever visited his corner of the city, it was for a formal-but-brief dinner.

As for friends, the divorce ensured that very few would stick around. Brittany had capably spun a tale to everyone who'd listen. Her version suggested that their marriage was riddled with infidelities and scandal. Their mutual friends and acquaintances naturally assumed it was he who cheated. He didn't care enough to correct them.

So, the second room slowly became an in-home office. Finally, Kurt committed to making it an extension of his work office. He moved his computer from his kitchen table to an industrial-style metal desk he'd ordered online. He added small touches with a vintage task lamp, a gaming chair, and some framed pop art.

Those elements, grounded by a braided black rug on the standard-issue carpet, did little to make it feel like home. It was simply a place to sleep until he could wake up, read the news, and get to work.

He logged into his password-protected desktop and jumped online. He tried a variety of combinations of search terms for Maplewood and Mary Delaney. He found the town on a satellite map, thankfully. He even found the weather for the mountain range, and it looked like snow all through the week and weekend. He made a mental note to toss in gloves and a scarf, if he could hunt them down.

Then he went back to a general search for Mary Delaney. Nothing. Finally, it occurred to him to scour social media. Tech-savvy though he was, Kurt didn't personally use social media. It seemed to him like nothing more than high school drama, playing out online behind the safety of a keyboard.

After no results on Mary, he had a better idea.

Surely Anna was the type to blog or socialize online.

Having no accounts himself, Kurt could only access publically-available results for "Anna Delaney." But, at the bottom of the first page of hits, he found her. He clicked on her thumbnail image and up came her profile. He was surprised to see that her entire profile was public. *Tsk, tsk,* he thought to himself. Anna should know better.

Kurt scrolled down her profile until he came across her friends list. He quickly typed "Mary" into the search bar but no match. He scrolled back up and found her online photo albums. All public. He leaned back, stretching his long arms in front him, then settled back in.

After clicking through two albums of seemingly random uploads of Anna at a few work events and Anna and her friends out for dinner and drinks, he came across what was apparently a family photo, based on the tags. In it, Anna was standing on the far left side of two rows of people. The two next to her looked significantly older than the others. They must be her parents.

Next to her parents were two men. Even taller than Anna (who came close to Kurt's height), they were surely well over six foot. One was red-headed like Anna, the other brown-haired.

In the front row were three women. One heavily pregnant, with long, straight blonde hair. The middle was decidedly not pregnant but had a muscular build and pretty face. They both had Anna's light eyes.

As Kurt's eyes moved to the last woman in the line, his breath caught and his jaw tensed. He leaned in a little closer to the screen. She was beautiful. Wild and comfortable-looking and beautiful. She was shorter than every other person in the picture. And her long, wavy brown hair fell every which way. She, too, had light eyes, but they seemed to look right back at Kurt, piercing the guard he had put up.

Kurt sat back, running a hand over the back of his neck. He closed the web browser and took a deep breath in, releasing it slowly. Could it be?

He stood and walked back to his bedroom where he left his phone on his bag. He grabbed the phone and composed a new text to Anna.

*I'd like to reach out to the innkeeper ahead of our trip to discuss some minor details. Can you help?*

His heart racing, he pressed send. Mixing work with pleasure was a risk. But he was starting to think he had nothing to lose.

# Chapter 11

The library was closed for a whole week, due to the weather. Fortunately, the snowfall had subsided by the following Wednesday, and the Mayor convinced the librarian to open for a couple of hours. At least, that's what Mary read in the newspaper as she was sipping on a cup of steaming black coffee at Zick's, Maplewood's most popular breakfast spot.

Mary had spent the past week cleaning the rest of the lodge and shoveling the parking spaces out front. It was a foolish thing to do since the local radio station clearly aired that snow was expected indefinitely. But, she felt better keeping busy, and at least it would mean less shoveling come Friday.

Before trying the library again, she decided to treat herself to a light breakfast out. That's when she came across the gossipy article in the extra Mountain News copy that Leslie Zick would leave out at the front counter.

Mary chuckled to herself as she read through Mayor Flanagan's supposed interview in the paper. In it, he defended Kathy Chisolm, the one-and-only librarian Maplewood had known in the past two decades.

Mary had first met Kathy in high school, when the librarian had visited the English classrooms to remind students of the luxury of having a local public library. While others mocked Kathy's effort, Mary had taken it seriously and even found herself dropping in to get a book here or there.

It was no surprise that Kathy didn't want to shovel her drive and dig her little sedan out only to show up at the library for people who weren't interested in the books anyway. All they wanted was to check their email or print something off the ancient black-and-white copy machine.

But Mary had to laugh when she realized that the Mayor was pressured into forcing Kathy to open the library despite the bad weather. Mary wondered who cared enough to put the heat on? No matter, she appreciated it. Even if it was a real hassle for poor Kathy.

Mary swallowed down another few sips before calling it good. She left behind a dollar on the white Formica dining table, knowing full well that if she tried to deposit it in the tip jar at the counter, that Leslie would fish it out and tuck into Mary's back pocket.

Though Mary didn't get out much, most of the locals knew her as the Delaney daughter who wanted to stick around. Sometimes, Mary wondered if the locals judged her for choosing to stay, instead of heading off to college or pursuing big city interests, but Mary didn't mind. She was happy to live in the same little town in which she grew up. She never wanted to leave, and she hoped she didn't have to.

As she pushed open the wooden door of the bakery, the bells overhead chimed. She looked up to see Leslie on a ladder just by the door. She was now starting to hang the Christmas lights. Leslie looked down at Mary, her hands gloved and head covered in a crocheted hat.

"About a week-and-a-half late, Mary. Don't tell your mom. I know she starts her decorations on Thanksgiving Day!" Mary smiled warmly, thinking of her sweet mother who would probably start Christmas preparations on the first of October if it weren't for society. But, her mother was as much a stickler for tradition as she was a lover of Christmas.

"I won't. I have only barely started myself," Mary replied, tucking her hands into her down jacket. "See you later, Les," she offered a parting smile as she sashayed toward her old, red jeep. Leslie waved goodbye from her precarious spot on the ladder and carried on in the important work of hanging lights.

As Mary climbed into her seat, she considered her options for the decoration activities Anna had suggested.

Mary planned to hang the lights later that day or tomorrow. She had already hung the wreath and set up the Nativity scene on the mantel. She'd woven garland around the banister and dangled a set of silver bells above the front door. She'd added some other miscellaneous pieces to the reception desk and the coffee table, but since the weekend was meant to be a professional retreat, she kept the mistletoe stowed safely in a bin. She didn't want to put anyone in an uncomfortable position.

Mary planned to have the guests make gingerbread houses for one activity. And she wanted them to trim the tree. But she still didn't know what to do about a tree.

As she turned the ignition, she sat, watching Leslie balance on the ladder as the jeep heated up. She thought about what she needed to do, and what her tree options were.

She could spend Thursday driving into the nearest city, Lowell, to shop for supplies. Maybe she could splurge and buy another imitation tree. Or, she could to go to her parents' house and beg her dad to go back out to the woods and cut another tree for her. Neither choice appealed to her, and she decided to wait until the next day to figure out that particular problem.

Still, Mary needed to stock up on some groceries anyway, and she was worried that Fred's Country Market would not carry everything she was planning to get. It made sense to make the journey over to Lowell today and get it out of the way.

As the air from the vents started to warm, Mary put the jeep in reverse and pulled out of Leslie's slushy gravel parking lot and onto the main drag.

Two blocks down, she turned right into the tiny library parking lot. It was also gravel, but instead of slush, it was crunchy with thick snow in some spots and icy in others. Mary decided to ask Kathy if she had any rock salt. It wasn't safe.

Upon parking, she dropped out of the jeep and slipped and slid her way up to the front door. She pulled it open and noted that Kathy must have barely arrived. It was still chilly inside the little two-room library.

"Kathy? It's Mary Delaney. Are you around?" Mary called into the empty space. Out popped Kathy's white curls from behind the farthest shelf.

"Oh, hello, Mary," she replied as she returned her attention to the shelves. Mary had no idea what she could be doing since re-shelving had all but become a lost art at the Maplewood Public Library.

"Do you want me to salt the walkways and the parking lot for you? It's pretty bad out, and I wouldn't want you to slip?" Mary called back as she moved toward the center table, which held the one computer in the library. She pressed the power button, knowing it would take a couple minutes to boot up.

"No, no. Bob Flanagan'll be along soon. That was part of the deal. If he can't get the town to plow here, then he better get his own butt on over here to do it himself, because the good Lord knows I ain't picking up a shovel at my age. And if they expect me to keep this place open in the cold of winter, then he knows to handle it his own self." As she finished, she hefted a stack of encyclopedias down onto the computer table. Mary smiled at the old librarian's spark. She loved how Kathy never put on airs, despite being probably one of the most educated women in town.

"What do you intend to do with those?" Mary gestured to the stack of reference books.

"Get rid of 'em. Why? Do you have any need for encyclopedias from the eighties? Because I sure as heck don't," Kathy harrumphed.

"Hmm, no. Well, Kathy, don't mind me. I just need to put together a little schedule and print out a couple copies. I won't be too long."

"No books?" Kathy's irritation grew.

"Oh, well. Sure. I'll take a look once I get the copy machine going," Mary agreed.

Once she got into the computer and pulled up a word processor, she typed out a simple itinerary with days, times, and suggested events. Nothing pushy. Meals, marshmallow roasting, gingerbread cabin-building, and tree-trimming. She still had to figure out the last item. She spent another few moments searching the clip art catalog for a little mistletoe or pine bough. All she could find was a single pine tree. But she liked that, so she added it to the top center of the page. She then sent ten copies to the printer before remembering to email one to her sister. As the copies were shuffling through the creaking plastic machine, she walked along the New Release section at the front shelf. She picked out a Jane Austen biography and set it at the circulation desk as she collected her pages. She then logged off, shut down the computer, and waited for Kathy.

"Alright, here we go," Kathy limped her way to the front desk. She looked over her bifocals at her own computer and scanned the book.

"Thanks, Kathy. Have a great day. Stay warm," Mary smiled to her and Kathy nodded back, a slight upturn of her mouth.

"You, too, dear."

With that, Mary was off to the city.

As she pulled out onto the road, she heard her cell phone chirp from its spot in her purse. She made it a rule to never look at her phone while driving, and in fact, she forgot all about the little chirp for the duration of the trip. It wasn't until she was unloading her groceries and boxes that evening that she pulled her phone out, aimlessly checking it for missed calls.

And there was the text from earlier. It was an unknown number, but Mary recognized the area code as the greater Phoenix area. She let her eyes skim the brief message.

*Is this Mary Delaney?*

# Chapter 12

Kurt wasn't sure if he had crossed the line by asking her for Mary's number. Usually, he did his absolute best to keep things professional in the office, and he didn't want to sully that reputation.

But, he reasoned, he was only human. And he had to know which sister of Anna's was running the inn. From a responsibility standpoint as a company owner, or so he told himself.

Was she the one in beat-up boots and ripped jeans? Wearing a red flannel sweater that accentuated her figure while somehow hiding it? He was dying to know. Kurt had never been a man who believed in love at first sight, but seeing that photo sparked something in him that he never felt with Brittany. Or any woman.

He and Britt had met at a frat party in college. She was gorgeous with white-blonde hair past her waist. She would later cut it into a crisp, trendy bob that further flattered her angular jaw. Kurt was always attracted to Brittany, no doubt. And she was as goal-oriented as he, studying hard in business school and going on to become the president at a major bank in Downtown Phoenix.

But as their marriage wore on, it turned out that Kurt and Brittany had dramatically different values. In college, she had convinced him she wanted children. By the time they married the year after graduating, she convinced him she would cut back on work and be home in time in for dinner, or at least for dessert. Five years after that, she convinced him that her late nights were only work-related. No funny business with one of the chairmen with whom she'd become close. Two years after that, she convinced him she would end things with the chairman and recommit to Kurt. Finally, after another two years, Kurt called it quits.

Filing for a divorce was the hardest thing he had done. To him, marriage was more than a contract. It was a pact. And Kurt was initially willing to do anything in order to make things work with Brittany. But it was during a mundane coffee date, at a time when she finally seemed to be coming back around to him, that he realized he just didn't love her. As she ignored his small-talk, he decided then and there that there was nothing to save. Even light questions about how she slept and if she wanted sugar or cream were too much for the relationship. Coming to this truth broke his heart and made him question everything about himself.

Soon after filing the divorce papers, he made the transition to promote his hobby, cryptocurrency, to his full-time gig. He contacted some friends from college who helped connect him to other tech-minded finance people. It was how he met Anna, in fact.

Once they got FantasyCoin off the ground, it took flight. The timing was perfect, and he had the right team. Once it became clear that FantasyCoin would be profitable, he was comfortable enough to dip into his substantial savings to buy a nice condo near his office.

From there, he decided to refocus. He didn't date. He had no interest. Most of his energy went to his growing business. Personal time was spent at the gym or reading self-help books.

On occasion, his college friends would invite him for a pick-up basketball game or a family barbeque. The latter only reminded him of his loneliness. He often thought about finding a girlfriend but had no interest in going to bars. One of his married friends suggested he try online dating. At first, that appealed to Kurt, who loved being online. But, ultimately, he couldn't bring himself to do it. He just wasn't ready.

All he could think about was his broken marriage with Brittany and how he had failed- either in selecting a mate or making his mate happy. So, he gave up. He hadn't felt that butterflies-in-the-stomach, car-going-over-a-quick-hill feeling in eons.

Until he saw Anna's family photo.

He prayed for that enchanting girl to be the same sister he'd be meeting in just two days. But he had to do more than pray. He had to act.

Which was why he texted Anna immediately. He needed Mary's phone number.

Her response was not surprising.

*Why*

No question mark. Just the one word. He decided to be honest with her.

*Came across a pic of your family. Just curious.*

36

He sucked in a breath. He wasn't sure where this would go. Would Anna shut him down? What if the picture wasn't even her family? What if Mary turned out to be that gorgeous girl, but she was married? Or not his type, even? Sure, he liked Anna enough as a coworker, but if Mary had a similar, dominating and impatient personality, he'd lose interest fast.

He had never gone out on a limb like this. He found himself staring at his phone screen. He anxiously dropped it onto his bed and paced his room. He ran his hand through his dark hair and let out another deep sigh.

He grabbed his phone again, trying to avoid looking at the screen. He took it into his bathroom and changed into a t-shirt and sweats. As he set the phone on the sink to brush his teeth, he assessed his stubble in the mirror. He was starting to like the look of it, so he decided to let it ride for the weekend in the woods. He hadn't grown a beard in years. It might be a nice change. Fresh start?

Just as his toothbrush clinked into its glass holder, Kurt's phone pinged. He snatched it up, opening the messaging app. The words glowed back at him.

*Stalking my family? Real professional, Kurt. If you think I'm going to set you up with my sister, fat chance. I'll give you her number for details for this weekend, fine. This is all on you. I don't want to be involved.*

Kurt felt a little panicked. He only got attitude from Anna when she was very upset. Maybe this was a mistake. And yet, she had given him the number.

He contemplated how to reply to Anna.

*Thanks, Anna.*

Short and sweet.

Not a moment later, his phone vibrated as he saw Anna's response. Ten digits. Nothing more. Nothing less.

With that, he grinned and headed to his bedroom.

# Chapter 13

Confused at first, Mary finally figured that cell phone scams were either ramping up, or this random person was one of her mother's unwelcome attempts at a set-up.

It wasn't the first time her mother had happened to meet an eligible bachelor either at church or in town on a grocery trip and passed on Mary's number.

Mary hated it. It made her feel like some sort of third party to her own love life. And the few men to whom Mary had responded were out-of-towners anyway. Flatlanders, as the locals would call them. City boys. Mary didn't know what her type was, yet, but she knew for a fact it wasn't a city boy.

She stuffed her phone into her jacket pocket, ignoring the intrusive text, and continued carrying in the groceries.

On her fourth and final trip, her cell phone rang. As she fumbled to pull it out she thought to herself that this was the exact reason that she usually left it plugged in upstairs. She hated being readily available 24/7. She checked the screen, and it was her mom, of all people. Clicking the green phone icon, she greeted her mother with impatience.

"Mom, was that you?"

"Was *what* me?" her mom answered.

"I mean the text I just got from a strange number. Is that your handiwork, by any chance?"

Her mother hardly paused. "No. What in the world are you talking about, Mary? I didn't text you any message. I don't think I can make a text from my landline here." Conversations with her even less tech-savvy parents could be mildly infuriating. In fact, these conversations were the exact reason that Mary forced herself to use a smartphone and register an email address at all. She might live simply, but she was definitely online and in touch.

"Mom, I meant did you give my number to someone again? I got a message from a number I don't know," Mary clarified.

"Oh." Margaret paused. "Why? Did the strange phone number ask you out on a date? Oh, Mary Beth Delaney, that could be wonderful! Say yes, please for my sake, say yes! For the Lord's sake, say yes!" Her mother was booming into the phone now.

"No one asked me on a date, Mom. Never mind. It must be spam." Mary breathed out a sigh of frustration before continuing. "Anyway, how are you all? Is everything okay?" Mary changed the subject, wondering why her mother was calling.

Phone calls between them had been rare and limited to specific issues, like was Mary joining them for church on Sunday or not? And did Mom have that recipe for Mountain Mac and Cheese? They may be irritated with each other on a regular basis. But wasn't that the foundation of a close-knit family, anyway?

"Oh, well. What a shame. Anyway, yes, your brothers and your daddy are taking the trucks out to the woods this weekend to cut down fir trees for Christmas. I know you have that big, plastic, fake tree, but we wanted to give you a chance to join us this year. The boys are happy to cut a tree for you, if you can haul it back to the lodge in your jeep."

Mary raised her eyebrow at the offer. Her mother had always supported anyone's efforts at over-the-top Christmas decorations, but she had almost altogether stopped supporting Mary's independence at the lodge.

For the past five Christmases, Margaret Delaney had continued to invite Mary to the farm for each of her exponentially grander events: decorating the farm, celebrating at the farm, and cleaning up at the farm. However, never did she offer to come do the same for the lodge.

For Margaret to invite Mary along to the sacred, men-only Christmas tree-cutting-down-ritual was strange. So strange, that Mary was suspicious.

"Oh, Mom. That is really sweet of you all," Mary started. "But, I can't." Which was true. "I actually got a group coming up this weekend for a," Mary paused, wondering if she ought to go into detail. She decided against it. "I mean I actually have some reservations for the weekend, and so I'm stuck here. But, I really do appreciate the offer."

"Suit yourself. I guess that means you won't be to church either?" Her mother's pouting voice carried enough guilt for the whole congregation.

"Mom, I wish I could. I really have to be at the Lodge around the clock.

"Hm, that's just too bad, Mary. I don't know what will become of you, sweetheart. I really worry for you, Mary Beth." The thick sugar in Margaret's voice had little effect on Mary, a seasoned veteran when it came to defending against the passive-aggressive pleading.

"No need, Mom. I'm really fine. I'm excited for this weekend; it could be great for business," Mary paused, holding her breath for some validation. When she heard a sigh on the other end, she wrapped the conversation up. "It was great hearing from you, Mom. Give the boys hugs for me. I'll see you soon. Promise." And with that, Mary gently ended the call.

Mary checked the clock, feeling tired and cold. She had let the fire go out before she had left that morning. Since she kept the thermostat at 62 degrees, it had been stuck there since that morning.

She was about to set the phone back down on the counter and return to groceries, when she saw the message notification clinging to the screen. She had almost entirely forgotten. She'd take care of this funny business right then and there. She had too much to do to deal with scammers.

*Wrong number. Delete me.* She hesitated, her good manners keeping her from sending.

*Please. Thank you.* She added, before pressing send and muting the phone.

# Chapter 14

Mary's response caught Kurt off guard. Wrong number? He re-checked Anna's text and cross-referenced the numbers between the two messages as well as he could. It was the same number. Did he dare text Anna back and ask her for the number again? Did he respond to the person at the "wrong" number? Did he simply sit and wait for the next 48 hours to pass so he could just see this woman in the flesh?

He sat back onto his bed and bit his nails while staring at the phone screen. He would simply sleep on it.

He decided instead to head back to his desktop and look at the weather again since he'd been too distracted before.

As he pulled up his browser, he felt tempted to go back to Anna's family picture. He forced himself not to.

Instead, he restarted his search for the weather on Maplewood Mountain. He wanted to double check it. He found the zip code for the area. Once he had it, he entered into his weather search app on his phone, and bingo. Up came Maplewood. The forecast looked dramatically different than his own. Snow all weekend.

It was like a different world. How could it be snowing only four hours away and in the same state? The high in Phoenix was slated to remain in the 70s all weekend.

It was the second week of December. People were gearing up for a white Christmas in most of the rest of the country, but not in Phoenix. He could see the appeal of having a "real" Christmas experience and understood why many of his friends would rent cabins in the mountains come Christmas vacation.

Then again, most of those rentals existed in the Northern most mountain ranges, not Maplewood. He figured that was because Maplewood was especially tiny.

He wondered if it even had many businesses at all. What industry sustained Maplewood? He did a quick web search for the town. One related hit. It was a very brief online encyclopedia entry citing the town's population, climate, and demographics. Climate was as expected- mountain forest with an average year-round temperature of 51 degrees.

The population was a mere 500, not including summer and winter tourist hikes, which would bring the total up to a suggested 700. Better make that 707, Kurt thought to himself. Because here we come.

With a renewed excitement, he again closed the browser and then shut the computer down. He decided he'd throw his old ski jacket into his duffle, only to realize it wouldn't fit. He would feel silly bringing any bigger of a bag, though.

With this, he felt an opportunity present itself. He would shoot Anna a follow-up text to ask about her packing plans and what to expect, weather-wise. After all, she was from Maplewood.

*Sorry to bother you again. Should I plan to pack for activities out in the snow? I've got warm clothes, but I don't know if I should add snow gear?*

He waited a minute, wondering if he should add his burning question. He decided against it and hit send. Not a minute later, Anna replied.

*That would be a good question for Mary. Why not ask her since you have a direct line now?*

Hm. Maybe Anna didn't mind too much if he was chatting up her sister. She gave him the opening, so he took it.

*I would, but the response I got was 'wrong number' . . .*

Kurt watched the screen, as Anna typed out a response. Worst case, Anna would tell him what to pack. Best case, he'd get the right phone number.

*Ha. Sounds like Mary. Good for her.*

Kurt was confused. "Good for her?" What was he missing? He considered asking for clarification, but Anna was clearly not interested in helping him. Still, he couldn't just let it go.

*Okay, well. Snow jacket? Gloves? Yay or nay?* He played it safe and stuck to his original question.

*I'll call her and get back to you. I'd say yay. Who knows what we are in for? Christmas theme, right?*

Kurt decided once and for all to just give it up. Anna was blocking his efforts, and he didn't even know if Mary and the green-eyed beauty were one and the same.

42

He couldn't get his hopes up. He did that once already. For over ten years. It didn't play out well for him. He put his phone to sleep and went to the spare room closet to grab his snow jacket and gloves. He set them beside his duffle, plugged his phone in, grabbed his book and settled into bed for the night. He had to let it go.

Half an hour later, his eyes grew heavy as his tired hands fumbled to dog-ear his current page.

He pulled his socks off, tucked himself under the covers and sleepily set his book on the nightstand next to the phone. Just after shutting off the lamp and closing his eyes, a new text appeared in his messages.

# Chapter 15

Mary was finally crawling under the white down comforter and into her cozy, iron-framed bed, tired from the busy day, but a little wired with excitement. She grabbed for the book she had checked out earlier.

Just as she flipped to the first page, her cell phone beeped. She had forgotten to mute it after plugging it in. She lifted herself up to peek at the screen. It was a new message from Anna. If there was anyone Mary was willing to text with late at night, it was her sister. She popped the charging cord off the bottom of the phone and leaned back onto her pillow, opening the message.

*Hey, are you up?*

Mary sighed. *Yeah?* She wrote back, anxiously hoping to answer Anna's question and get back to her book. She needed something to put her to sleep, and though she was interested in the Austen biography, it would certainly help to quell her racing mind.

Mary thought about the fact that she had the unique ability to fall in love with any book she picked up. If only this ability would translate to her love life.

*Did you get a text earlier today?*

Mary abruptly sat up. How did Anna know? It made no sense. Anna was not the sort to give out Mary's number. Maybe there was an issue with the retreat? Or maybe one of the employees just had a question Anna couldn't answer?

*Oh, dang. Yeah. I wrote it off as the wrong number. Is everything okay? Is it about the retreat?*

She watched as her sister took a moment to type back.

*Everything is fine, except my boss, who is usually cool, is trying to hit on you. Good for you for ignoring him. That's the sister I know and love!*

Mary read her sister's response twice. What had Anna meant? Frustrated by the slow process of texting, she clicked on her sister's name and called her directly.

Anna picked up right away. "Hey. You were right to ignore him, don't sweat it. I just wanted to check in and let you know that Kurt is totally cool. I have no idea why he actually wanted your number, but knowing men, he probably wanted to scope you out for the weekend. He'll get over it."

Mary needed her to back up. "Anna, what are you talking about? The person who texted me is *Kurt?*" Anna was bewildered by this.

"Yeah, he asked for your number to check in with you ahead of this weekend. He claims he saw a picture of you. I gave him your number, but don't worry, Mary. I told him I'm not setting you up. First of all, despite Mom's desperate efforts, you don't need a man to be happy. Second of all, if I were going to endorse someone for your romantic interests, it would NOT be Kurt. He's divorced and hyper-focused on work. He's got no personal life, either. I was shocked that he wanted your number at all." Anna finished her spontaneous lecture.

Mary had long ago accepted that her sister was almost always hyper-judgmental of men, even ones she respected. She never wanted to get married. Instead, she preferred to use men. It was like she was on a mission to prove something, though Mary couldn't figure out what.

"Okay, let me get this straight. Your boss asked for my number, and you assumed he wanted to hit on me? But you didn't tell me about this exchange, and instead, let me embarrass myself and compromise my professionalism. Because, Anna, that is exactly what I did." Mary frowned and crossed her free arm under the one crooked at her ear. Mary knew, in her heart, that Anna had good intentions. But sometimes Anna's sense of justice and moral high ground got in the way of decency. Mary waited for Anna's response, which finally came on the heels of an exaggerated sigh.

"Okay, well, sorry for trying to help. I don't want to see you get your hopes up that some city boy is going to come rescue you from your little lodge life in Maplewood. You're doing just fine, and this weekend will help. I'm protecting you." Anna stopped.

"Protecting me from what? Your boss texting me to get information on his company trip? And anyway, you *like* Kurt. You talk about how smart he is and how he respects you and his employees. So if he *is* trying to hit on me, which by the way makes no sense since we haven't even met, so what? That doesn't mean I'm going to get swept up in some big city fantasy that I decidedly do not have. And speaking of that," Mary was getting heated, "I don't have a small life here. I have a good life. Maybe I don't have a strong business, yet. Maybe I don't have a boyfriend or a husband or a string of one-night-stands to make me feel good about myself. Maybe I barely even have the support of my family. But I'm hanging in there."

Mary was on a roll and couldn't stop. "You're no better than Mom. You pressuring me in the exact opposite direction doesn't help. I will figure things out on my own, and for you to suggest that I'm a miserable old spinster really undermines your goal anyway, Anna." There. She said it. She said everything she was thinking and then some. It was true that Mary didn't know what she wanted. It was true that she felt pressure from all sides.

To think that Anna's boss was interested in her was laughable. Not only had he never met her, but they could not be any more different. Even Mary and Anna were worlds apart. The only thing they had in common was their last name, really.

Mary was starting to wonder how she and Anna had even managed to stay as close as they had through the years. Were they both lonely? Clinging to the only relationship that seemed to be lasting for them- sisterhood?

She heard Anna shift on the other end of the line, so she continued to push back. "Well, Anna? What's the deal? Is this weekend going to work out, or is there going to be a problem with the fact that your boss simply wanted to get in touch with the person who is running his work event? Because it seems like a problem is now forming since you left me to reply to him like a real jerk."

She heard Anna stifle a chuckle. "Mary, what did you say, anyway?"

"I told him he had the wrong number, basically," Mary replied.

"Sometimes, Mary, you're even feistier than me." Anna joked into the phone, clearly trying to make amends, even in a small way. Mary still felt slighted by her sister's assumptions and judgments.

"Doesn't matter. I already made a fool of myself. I guess I'll write him back and clear that up. I don't want him to think the retreat isn't legitimate," Mary complained.

"Listen, Mary, I'm sorry. I didn't mean to suggest that you're not happy. I just want you to be happy, and I can feel your loneliness sometimes," Anna paused before going on. "But you know what? I have a feeling that's all about to change. I think this retreat might completely up your level of success at the lodge. It'll be a great trial, at least, you know?"

"Yeah, I agree," Mary muttered back.

"Okay, well, sis don't worry about Kurt. His male ego can take the hit of being spurned a bit, even if he had no romantic motives. You'll meet him soon enough. I think all he wanted to know was how to plan for the weather, anyway." Anna's voice evened out.

"Okay," was all Mary could offer. The sisters ended the phone call, and Mary slid back down beneath the covers, gripping her phone between her hands and thinking about what a successful businesswoman would do next.

# Chapter 16

The next morning, Kurt awoke slowly, nearly forgetting the events of the night before. As he dragged himself out of bed and into the kitchen for coffee, he started to recall his stupid text to Anna, igniting a now-embarrassing exchange between himself and his colleague.

He cringed a little as he scooped coffee beans from the bag into the grinder. Pressing the button, he resolved not to mention it at work and just pretend it didn't happen. He moved to the fridge to pull out eggs and butter.

He whipped himself up some scrambled eggs to go with his fresh-brewed coffee. Before he sat down to eat, he pulled open his front door to grab the daily paper from the doormat. He snapped off the rubber band and shook it up to the business section, before settling down to enjoy breakfast.

After finishing, he went to the bathroom to take a quick shower. He brushed his teeth, added a little gel to his thick, dark hair, mostly to keep it out of his face, and then he added deodorant and a dash of cologne.

Kurt strode back to his room and got dressed. He told the office that Thursday could be this week's casual Friday since they weren't working Friday. So, he pulled out his fitted jeans. He still wore a button-down, but he left the top button undone and rolled up the sleeves.

Finally, he slid into his brown, leather sandals. He grabbed his sunglasses from his dresser and his phone from its charging spot and, without glancing at it, headed back to the entryway, where he picked up his keys from the side table.

He flipped the lights off and headed down the elevator and to the basement parking lot. Kurt's building was one of few in Downtown Phoenix that had below-ground parking. He loved it, largely because he hated having to walk across black asphalt on a 110-degree day in the summer. Sweating in your work clothes before even arriving at work was an instant day-ruiner. Plus, opting for a leather interior in his car had been a bad choice.

When he finally got situated in his black, full-sized sedan, he drew his phone up to see that he had an unread message. He panicked for a moment, thinking it might be Anna, condemning him further for inquiring about Mary. He clicked on the message and froze.

It was Mary, after all.

*Kurt, I'm so sorry about my earlier message. Just talked to Anna, and she told me she gave you my number. I assumed your text was spam. Again, so sorry. I'm happy to answer any questions you have about this weekend. Thanks. -Mary.*

Kurt felt his heart rate double, instantly. His hands even started to sweat a little. He realized he hadn't started the car, and quickly pressed the ignition button and muted the stereo. Then, he looked back down at the message and hurriedly typed a response.

*Mary, hey! No worries. Just wanted to touch base and let you know my team is excited to stay at your lodge for the weekend.*

He paused and looked up at the concrete wall in front of him, then side to side to see if anyone was watching him sit in his car with a silly grin on his face. When he saw that the coast was clear, he finished typing.

*If there is anything you can think of that we ought to pack, please let me know. Most Arizonans don't always have a clue about cooler climates.*

He read back over the text, looking for errors. Seeing none, he hit send and punched the car into reverse, tucking the phone between his legs.

He didn't get as far as the exit gate before he felt the phone vibrate. He looked into his rear view to check if anyone was behind him, and two cars were there, waiting for him to move up.

Kurt was nothing if not a safe driver, so he pulled forward through the exit and then off to the little side road before the traffic light. As he put the car back into park, he excitedly clicked on Mary's message.

# Chapter 17

*Good morning! Well, that's a great question. You'll probably want to pack winter clothes and maybe even something for the snow. It's been steadily coming down and the forecast predicts lots more. We will be outside a bit, too.*

Mary pressed send.

Feeling like she had resolved the matter, she crawled out of bed and tucked her feet into her slippers on the floor. She stretched up and then, feeling giddy, flopped back down the bed.

She had slept great, and today was the day before the FantasyCoin team arrived. It almost felt like Christmas Eve, like something magical was about to happen.

She bounced back up, surprisingly wide-eyed, and walked into her en-suite bathroom, which was even chillier than the lofty bedroom. She pushed the door in to grab her robe from the back of it. Her robe had seen better days. It was starting to tatter at the hem, cuffs, and collar, but it was comfy and warm. She pulled it onto her quivering body and pranced out of the room and padded down the stairway.

On into the kitchen she pranced, where she pulled out her canister of coffee grounds. She set the coffee to drip, poured in a small scoop of grounds and realized she left her phone on her bed.

She scrambled back up the stairs and snatched it off her comforter. As she skipped back down to the kitchen, she unlocked the screen to see that she had missed Kurt's response. She noted that her phone hadn't had this much action maybe ever, and smiled as she pulled up the new text.

*Sounds good. Although, I doubt if any of us have real snow gear. Haha.*

Mary appreciated that Kurt was the sort to type out "haha." It made her feel comfortable, for some reason.

*Don't worry. It's not like we will be chopping down pine trees in the woods. And just as she hit send, a thought occurred to her.*

50

Cutting down trees. Team building. Christmas tree. It could work. But first she'd have to correct her statement, and secondly, she'd have to make sure she had the supplies necessary.

She waited a beat to think about if it could work. It was the perfect culminating event. Maybe they could even form two teams and create a competition of it. Winner got a prize basket or something. Maybe she could include gift certificates to Zick's. It had to work. It was a cool idea, and Mary knew that it would be interesting for the team. Maybe hard. But interesting. Something a little edgier than gingerbread cabins. She typed out a correction text to Kurt.

*Actually, I take that back. There is a good chance we will be cutting trees. So, you might want to tell your people to pack for the occasion. And thanks for the great idea!*

Grinning widely, she pushed send and breezed into the kitchen, feeling energized. She set her phone down and poured herself a bowl of quick oatmeal and splashed in some milk. She didn't mind it cold and gobbled it up as she surveyed the kitchen.

The kitchen was open to both the great room and the formal dining room, but the dining room and great room were sort of partitioned by the see-through fireplace. The dining room was a nice size and fit a massive old farmhouse table that had been left behind by the previous owners. Weekly oiling kept it in good enough shape. Mary loved it and the two benches on either side. All she had left to clean was the kitchen and dining room, and they didn't need much since Mary already did a once-over after the past weekend's guests.

When the coffee drip had finished filling the glass carafe, she poured herself a mug and added two teaspoons of sugar. She then picked back up her phone to see that Kurt had responded already. He was efficient, that was for sure.

*We sure will. Thanks for the tip, Mary. I really look forward to meeting you.*

Mary felt herself blush slightly and inexplicably. She didn't understand why her pulse quickened with what was nothing more than a polite text response.

Maybe she really did need a little more interaction.

She thought about how to reply for a minute and then decided to keep it simple.

51

*I look forward to meeting you too, Kurt.* And then, since flattery never hurt anyone, she added: *I've heard great things about you.*

# Chapter 18

Kurt barely made it to work on time. He found himself pulling over twice more just to read Mary's messages. He didn't even *really* know what this woman looked like. He didn't know her at all. And yet, these little text exchanges were enthralling him. He could hardly focus on the road. Was he this desperate for a woman? Was it something else?

He had no idea, but he couldn't let himself get so wrapped up in a fantasy that would do nothing but distract him from what was meant to be a work retreat. A productive and relaxing work retreat. He had to keep his eyes on the prize: ensuring that his FantasyCoin team had enough energy and passion to make it through the holidays, when they were all but certain to have a financial slump.

Once he got into the building, he took the stairs up to the third floor. He needed to expend a little of this extra energy.

As he landed on the third floor, he pushed open the access door and walked the short hallway to FantasyCoin's offices.

As he entered, he noted he was exactly one minute early, which to him was at least nine minutes late. He took in the office and saw that everyone had beat him. He pushed away his embarrassment and instead called out, "Hey guys, good morning! It's the last day before the big retreat! Let's make this day count and get out of here at a reasonable hour." Anna and Maci smiled and nodded their heads. Eddie and Rory did a fist bump, as usual. The others muttered a quick agreement and settled in at their desks.

Kurt decided against stopping to talk to Anna and instead beelined for his own workstation.

As he eased into his slimline, black swivel chair, he surreptitiously pulled his phone out of his pocket and reread Mary's last message. He scratched his stubble as the phone rested on his left thigh. He left it there as he booted up his computer and navigated to his email, opening a couple more tabs and a spreadsheet.

Out of the corner of his vision, he noticed his phone screen go black, and he stirred it back to life. As he re-read for the fifth time what she wrote, he decided he needed to be the one to end the conversation, not her. That was the gentlemanly thing to do. Hunching over his lap, he began typing out a response when he was interrupted.

"Ahem?" He shot straight up, knocking his phone to the floor. Anna was standing in front of his desk, arms crossed, face flat.

"Hi, Anna," he greeted her as he reached down to pick up his phone, discreetly clicking the side button to put it back to sleep.

"Hey, Kurt. Listen. I'm sorry about all of last night's texting stuff and my sister and all that. Okay?" She was looking at the space to his right, clearly avoiding any eye contact. Kurt wondered why she seemed nervous now, when her texts last night were obviously firm.

"What do you have to be sorry about?" He asked her, leaning back in his chair and gesturing to the one in front of his desk.

She sat and looked squarely at him. But, she kept quiet, forcing him to carry the conversation. "I'm the one who should apologize, Anna. I realize how my text must have sounded. I hope you know that I truly am excited for the team this weekend. I might have gotten a little carried away with reaching out to Mary. I promise you that I'll be cool."

"Actually, Kurt," she started, "I really do need to be the one to apologize. To you *and* Mary, but I already talked to her last night. I assumed the worst of you, and that was both unprofessional and rude. And I also assumed my sister wouldn't appreciate it if you reached out to her. I was way wrong. I guess it's okay to open up a little here." She stopped, waiting for Kurt's encouragement.

"Oh, of course. Anna, I know I have made clear that business is business, but I hope you agree that FantasyCoin is a comfortable and friendly environment? I mean, I see the others act that way. You can too, you know," he assured her.

"Yes, you're right. And I am totally comfortable here. Where I am a little uncomfortable, I suppose, is my family life." Anna looked down at her hands for a beat. "I sometimes feel like I have to be my sister's protector, despite the fact that she really doesn't need that. She's a tough girl. I mean, to be frank, when I set up this retreat, I did it in part for all the reasons I gave you. I think it will be great for our team. But I also did it

54

for her. I don't want to undermine her credibility in any way, but you should just know that I love Mary very much, and I sometimes get a little pushy on her behalf." She looked back up and met his gaze.

"You know Anna," Kurt started as he leaned onto his desk, fixing his elbow on there and resting his jaw on his hand. He looked right at her. "I did not have a close-knit family growing up. I mean, for starters, I'm an only child. And, you probably know this, my parents are divorced. I really respect that you and your sister are close." He smiled tightly.

She smiled back. "Okay, well. I feel better about it. Let's just have fun this weekend, right?" She started to stand and smooth her hands down her slacks.

"Absolutely," Kurt set his phone up on the desk and moved to stand with her. Anna turned to go, but he stopped her. "Anna, wait. I do have to admit one small thing." She turned and look back, lifting her right eyebrow in question.

"I, uh, that picture I saw of your sister? Online? Last night. It's a big part of why I asked for her number," Kurt looked down awkwardly. He felt better being upfront with Anna, but he was uncomfortable.

She frowned in response, forcing him to explain himself. "But I meant what I said. I did need more info on packing for the mountains," he chuckled at the last of what he said.

"What picture?" Anna asked, reaching for the chair back.

"On your social media page. I just sort of fell down the rabbit hole of looking up Maplewood and the Lodge, and that's as far as I could really get. Your sister truly is off the grid. Or, at least, offline. I have to admit that it piqued my interest."

"Kurt, I don't care. It's fine, really," her tone evened out, to his relief. "Let's just move on." And with that, she turned to head back to her desk, leaving Kurt to wonder if Anna was disappointed in him. Sure, he and Anna had only had a professional relationship, but everyone on the team was very, very open with one another. Maci and Rory had even gone out on a couple dates over the summer. It wasn't too farfetched for any one of them to be somehow involved in another's love life.

He couldn't help that he was excited to meet Mary. And the last thing he wanted was to pretend he wasn't. Kurt was nothing if not an honest person. But Kurt was also the boss.

His gaze followed Anna to her desk, and he sighed heavily, wondering if he should have kept his mouth shut. Once she started to get to work, he remembered the text he was about to write. As he began typing back to Mary, a new message appeared on his phone. It was from Anna. He clicked it.

*By the way. If you were wondering, here's a more recent photo of Mary.*

Kurt's head shot up at Anna, who was grinning mischievously at him.

# Chapter 19

Mary had spent the morning hanging Christmas lights around the front and back decks. When she had completed that, she took to oiling the dining table.

Finally, by about ten o'clock, she began to rummage around in the drawers of the baker's rack for her kitchen Christmas decor, which she would never stow in the dusty old storage shed.

Upon locating the carefully-rolled table runner and two small boxes of decorations, she hefted it all onto the table. She first unfurled the runner delicately down the middle. It hung off each side nearly a foot, its beige and red checkers adding life to the old wooden surface.

Then, she pulled out the two large, glass jars filled with pine cones. Some old gold glitter sat in the bottom of each jar, which maybe looked a little silly, but Mary didn't mind. *Character.* As her mother would say.

After the jars, she found her squat, wooden Christmas tree centerpiece, which she positioned right between the jars. Robert had made the tree in woodshop when he was in high school. Mary had a vague memory that it was meant for their mother, but somehow it appeared among Mary's things once she set up shop in the Lodge.

In the second box was a rope of garland, which Mary wove along the runner and between the decorations.

At last, she stepped back to the baker's rack and opened the top drawer, where she kept tablecloths, placemats, and fabric napkins. She shuffled below the top stack to find the winter collection beneath. It was a set she had sewn herself when she was just starting out at the lodge.

The placemats were deep red, thick, and over-sized. The napkins she had made out of a gingham material, which clashed with the table runner. Still, she thought the different patterns and textures added something special to her table setting.

After laying out each mat she folded the napkins into triangles, as her mother taught her when she was a child. She set the napkins square in the middle of the mats, where they would wait for plates.

Mary stepped back and admired her work. It was missing something. She moved back farther, almost bumping into the fireplace hearth.

It was the baker's rack. It was bare. She brought her hand to her mouth, running the pad of her index finger along her bottom lip as she thought.

Then, she spun on her heel and headed into the kitchen, where she found the step ladder. She moved it to the far cabinets and climbed up. On top of the cabinets, she kept the fancier mixing bowls, serving bowls and trays, and even some china. She pulled down the serving bowls and trays and moved back down the ladder.

After setting the serving collection into the sink to soak, she went to the large cabinet, where she kept guest dinnerware. She pulled eight dinner plates, eight bread plates, eight bowls, and eight mason jars (she had never bought a drinking glass in her life). As the serving items soaked, she took the plates, bowls, and jars to the side table, preparing them for use tomorrow. She returned to the kitchen and pulled her flatware organizer from its drawer and took it back to the dining room. Sashaying around the table, she set out the forks, spoons, and knives.

Finally, Mary returned for the serving bowls, rinsed and dried them, and brought them back to the long surface of the baker's rack, where she propped the various pieces behind the plates and bowls.

Stepping back again, Mary still wasn't satisfied. The framed picture of a snowy meadow behind the table added a backdrop and light. The low, rustic chandelier that hung above the table needed a wipe-down. But that wasn't it.

The space needed something other than the warmth of the runner and placemats. More than the sheen of the dinnerware. It needed drama.

She snapped her fingers and bounded over to and up the stairs, heading to her own bedroom. Once in there, she pulled to a stop at the antique dresser she'd brought from home. She opened the bottom drawer and pulled out two pewter candle holders and candlesticks. Cradling them in her arms, she trotted back down the steps and to the dining room. Mary carefully propped them up on either end of the side table.

The candles had been gifts to Mom and Dad for their wedding, but Mary begged to use them for her inaugural weekend at the Lodge, and her mom agreed to loan them. Perhaps Mom even forgot about them. But Mary hadn't. At the time, she thought they were good luck. Maybe that would be true again. Smiling at the beautiful setting, she placed her hands at the small of her back and bent back in a stretch. Perfect.

It was nearly lunchtime, and she wanted to be completely ready by dinner, so that she could spend the evening relaxing in the bath with a glass of the wine she splurged on.

She still needed to get some of the meals prepped, clear the campfire, and set up the hot cocoa station. After a quick peanut butter sandwich, she set about organizing.

First, she went outside to the little campfire circle that lay out back. She counted the stocky logs that formed the seating. Realizing she needed two more seats, she scanned the yard. She saw no other chunky chair-logs, as her dad called them.

As she scanned the area, she noticed a thick, felled pine tree peeking out from the snow about ten yards into the woods. She stomped her way over to get a better look. It would make for the perfect bench.

She pulled her mittens out of her jacket pocket and put them on. She then dragged the log over to fire, moving back the other stumps to make way for the double seater.

The fire pit was clear and ready for fresh logs. But since it continued to snow off and on, she decided to leave the logs on the deck instead of pre-arranging them like she had planned to.

Once she was satisfied with the little seating area, Mary went back to the kitchen to gather the hot cocoa supplies.

She neatly situated a jar for the cocoa powder, thermos for the hot water, and two glass dishes- one for the peppermint bark and one for marshmallows.

Mary had all the fixings for the gingerbread houses, but she decided to leave them in their little boxes since the tree-cutting may end up taking their place.

By the time she finished various other chores, it was nearing four o'clock. She sighed out a deep, contented breath and did a walk-through of the entire property, starting at the entrance from the highway. Few cars buzzed by as she plodded up the long drive, through the snow, and onto the front deck.

Though it was still a good hour until sunset, the overcast skies allowed the Christmas lights to glow. It looked beautiful.

Other than the lights, Mary had little exterior work to do. That was the benefit of snow. It made everything feel clean. She made her way into the lodge. The reception area was polished and pretty, the hot cocoa bar inviting, the fireplace cleaned out and set to go with three fresh logs inside. The dining room was radiant.

Mary ran her hand along the wooden banister as she moved upstairs and reviewed each guest room. Though simple, they, too were perfectly ready. Their flannel wool blankets added warmth to the pinewood tongue-and-groove walls and ceiling. She had even stocked the bathrooms with little homemade soaps from the farmer's market. Fluffy white towels and washcloths puffed out from their racks.

Mary walked back down the stairs, breathing in the place. It smelled like fresh pine needles and cinnamon. A smile spread across her face.

But then, she noticed the front hall closet and something occurred to her. The Christmas tree! THAT was where she had stuffed it last year. She skipped down the rest of the stairs and went to the open the door. Sure enough, there it was: skimpy and dull, leaning into the corner of the little closet. She stood back, remembering her other plan- to have the tree-cutting contest. But she had totally forgotten about securing the hand-saws, and by now it was too late to go into town or even down to the farm to borrow one from her parents.

Or was it? She was desperate. She didn't have a choice. She patted her jacket pockets for her phone, finding them empty but for her dirty mittens. Instead, she went to the reception desk and used the landline to dial up the farm.

Her mom answered after one ring. Fortunately, the conversation was short and sweet. Yes, Mary could borrow four hand saws. They needed to be returned by Monday morning.

She grabbed her keys from the hook by the reception desk and decided to drive down now and get it over with. Before she left, she wanted to take her phone, just in case.

She glanced around the room, not seeing it at reception or the hot cocoa table. She remembered she'd had it in the kitchen, so she went in there and found it where she had used it that morning- on the counter.

She had missed two texts. One from Kurt's number, which she ended up saving last night, and one from Anna.

She chose Kurt's first. *See you for dinner tomorrow!* She smiled. She liked that he had been the one to "finish" the conversation. It felt... right.

She then moved back to the home screen, before remembering to read Anna's. She opened the message. As her eyes floated across Anna's words, Mary's heart dropped.

*Talked to Kurt this AM. All's well. I think he has a crush on you, after all. LMAO. Men.*

# Chapter 20

The rest of Thursday had dragged by at a snail's pace. And by the end of it, Kurt could hardly fall asleep. He was anxious to get to Maplewood. Anxious to see what the team thought of it. Anxious to meet Mary.

Stunning Mary with her striking green eyes and wild mane. The picture Anna had sent confirmed Kurt's suspicions and made him feel weak.

Mary was a different beauty than any he'd known. Brittany, of course, had been conventionally attractive, with her firm, lithe body, bright blonde hair, and makeup applied just so.

But Mary had something indescribable. In the picture, Kurt saw contradictions: simple, but interesting. Untamed, but feminine. And she was clearly fit, but her curves suggested that hugging her was a soft, comfortable joy.

He had referenced back to the photo at least one hundred times through the day and on into the night and then even here and there in the wee hours of Friday morning before finally falling to sleep somewhere around four am.

A few hours later, he slowly awoke and dragged himself out of bed and directly into his shower. He could take his time since he wasn't meeting the others at the office until eleven, for a catered lunch. He wanted to kick the weekend off right, so he had ordered a few subs, sides, and drinks.

As soon as he finished showering, Kurt prepped his coffee machine and then went back to his room. He originally intended to wear a button-down and khaki slacks for traveling up to Maplewood. But after seeing Mary's picture, he changed his mind.

He didn't want to look like a lame tech nerd. He wanted to fit in. Kurt had a generic business style, but he had never thought much of it before.

So, as his coffee brewed, he scoured his closet until he found, peeking out in the way back, a long-sleeved tee shirt he had in college. It had a comfy look to it, including some deep wrinkles. So, he took the shirt to the bathroom and dampened it in the shower. He then tossed it into the dryer.

He pulled his second pair of jeans, which were more relaxed in their fit. He tied the jeans off with a brown belt and slid his feet into his tennis shoes, instead of his business-casual loafers.

Finally half-dressed, he popped the door open to grab the paper and strode back to the kitchen and scanned the different sections while sipping at his black coffee. Soon enough, the dryer buzzed and he set his mug and paper down to go retrieve the shirt. He pulled it out.

Tugging the shirt on, Kurt went back into his bedroom and snatched up his phone. He had noticed that there were no new calls or texts. He opened his calendar to review the plan one last time. Meet at the office at eleven, eat at 11:30, on the road by 12:30.

After doing another quick catalog of his duffle bag, he took his time in making his bed. He unplugged his cell charger and tossed it into the duffle then dropped the duffle by the entry way and dipped back into the kitchen to whip up some breakfast. He took his time, savoring the eggs and toast as he read the paper cover to cover and finished the rest of his coffee.

He left his condo in plenty of time and ended up beating the others by twenty minutes.

Once he unlocked the office door, he went to the supply room, where he found the long folding table. He brought it out to the open area in front of his own desk and popped out the legs.

He stationed himself by the window to watch for the food delivery van and took his phone out, opening it to his music app.

He settled on an old standby of his: Techno Chill. He wasn't sure if others appreciated his quirky music tastes, so he set it at a low volume and propped his phone on the edge of his desk, out of the way.

Finally, the others began to trickle in and recline at their own desks.

"Hey, hey, Happy Retreat Day, Boss!" Eddie called from the front door as he slid through, wearing a sweatshirt and jeans. Kurt was glad he decided to go casual, too.

"Hey, Eddie," Kurt replied, standing to high five him.

The others quickly followed, and by fifteen past the hour, the office was buzzing with excited chatter.

"Okay. Seriously, Kurt," Maci interrupted the group's discussion on snow and the impending winter drive. "I'm hijacking the music. I have no clue what station you've put on, but we are all in need of Christmas music. Duh," Maci giggled and Anna joined in.

"Alright, alright. It didn't even occur to me," Kurt half-heartedly defended himself. "It's all you, Mace," he clicked out of his phone's radio and let Maci take over.

"Men!" Maci interjected and she gave Anna a meaningful glare.

"Men. Indeed!" Anna called back and held up her Styrofoam cup to toast to Maci's joke.

Maci masterfully pulled out her own phone, swiped this way and that, and soon enough, "Silver Bells" was ringing through the office.

Kurt eyed his team members. No matter what happened when he met Mary, this trip was already great. He had never seen the office so full of cheer.

# Chapter 21

Mary had tossed and turned all night. Sleeping was impossible after Anna's shocking text.

Anna had only ever referred to Kurt in the most sterile terms. Boss this. President that. Founder. CEO. Crypto. FantasyCoin. The Team. Investments. Tokens. Conference calls.

In fact, before this week, it had never occurred to Mary that there was a real man behind all the business gibberish Anna used.

But slowly, very slowly, one was starting to form. She spent the early evening hours cataloging what she knew about Kurt. He was polite in his text messages. He was divorced. He was focused on work; he had to be in order to be as successful as he was. He was obviously a high-tech type. City guy.

He must respect Anna a lot because there had been many times that Anna mentioned to Mary how much Kurt relies on her.

And yet one thing stood out as a question. Why wasn't he interested in Anna?

She spent the midnight hours thinking of reasons to explain why Kurt and Anna hadn't hit it off romantically. Or had they? Assuming they had not, she first figured that Anna was not interested in him.

Anna, in fact, was not actually interested in any man. Not really. She chewed men up and spat them out, and she was too smart to get involved with someone at work.

Maybe Kurt was also not interested in her and for those very same reasons. Mary thought she could fall asleep after resting her case, but then she started picturing what Kurt might look like.

By two o'clock in the morning, she was so desperately curious that she cursed herself for not having reliable Internet at the Lodge. She never had as burning an urge to search for something, or someone, than she had that night.

Finally, by 2:30, she thought to use her phone. She often forgot it was a mini computer and that she could use her data to get online.

She twisted over to her nightstand and practically broke the phone off its charger as she frantically pulled up a search engine and began to type in his name. That was when she realized she didn't know his last name.

Fortunately, she was smart enough to simply search "Kurt, FantasyCoin." Pages of results instantly materialized. The first result was a biographical piece on some tech blog, complete with his picture and full name: Kurt Cutler. And he looked every bit of that name.

In the photo that accompanied the article, he was sitting back in an office chair, holding one ankle up on top the other leg. He looked different from pretty much every man she had ever met in person.

His dark hair was stylishly cut close on the sides and long on top with gel positioning it up and over to the side. His olive skin was clean-shaven. His blue eyes piercing. He looked to be tall and lean. He had full, smooth lips to match his hands, one of which was splayed out in front of him as if he was asking a question during the interview.

He was incredibly attractive, that was undeniable to Mary. But so much about him seemed wrong. His shirt and pants were cut closely to his body, probably the result of careful tailoring and styling. His tie was thin and popped off his chest in a vibrant orange, matching the textured dress socks that peeked out from the one pant leg.

After careful examination, she realized what it was. He wasn't like the guys she knew and loved. Not her dad, not her brothers. Not anyone she had ever dated. With that realization, Mary felt a swell of disappointment fill her, and she sadly closed out of the browser and put her phone to sleep. She, too, felt sleepy enough to try to close her eyes again.

Before she knew it, it was morning and the sun was peeking through a slit in the curtains to her bedside. Mary's excitement returned as she sprang out of bed. Today was the day she would revive Wood Smoke Lodge. In fact, it was a rebirth: The New Maplewood Retreat at Wood Smoke Lodge.

Leaving her phone behind on the table, she grabbed her tattered robe from her bathroom, swung it on, and glided down the stairs to pour some oatmeal.

After a quick breakfast, she carried a fresh mug of coffee back upstairs. She had gotten up a little after eight and wanted to be dressed and ready by late morning in order to give herself time to prep dinner, dessert, and the 'smores station.

She wanted to look put-together and professional, so she spent a solid half an hour in the shower lathering, conditioning and rinsing. She then took the time afterward to diffuse her hair, which helped bring out the waves without frizzing her long tresses.

She took another twenty minutes to forage through her old makeup bag and apply the bare minimum: some concealer, blush, mascara, and lip gloss. She tossed the lip gloss onto her bed for later.

Then, she went to her little closet. She hadn't decided what to wear yet. In fact, she had been dreading this part of Friday morning. She had precious few "professional" outfits. This was largely because Mary never knew how a good innkeeper really dressed. Especially one who ran a mountain lodge. As she rifled through the hangers, she realized her selection was going to make the decision for her.

She opted for the jeans and a deep red pullover sweater with a little hood. It was a thin sweater, which she preferred if she was going to be stoking the fire.

Finally, she fumbled around on the floor of the closet for her work boots. They were broken-in leather lace-ups and she loved them. She pulled them over a set of red cotton socks, not minding that her pant legs poked into and out of the boots, partly exposing the socks.

She lazily laced up the boots and tucked in the ends around the back, stood up and gave herself a once over in the mirror she had fastened on the back of her bedroom door. She was pleased. She looked like... well, she looked like herself. Fresh and happy.

# Chapter 22

The team had finished cleaning up the lunch leftovers by a little after noon, putting them into their convoy and on the road well before 12:30. They had split themselves into smaller carpools- Kato, Eddie, and Rory in Kato's car; Alex and Jace in Alex's SUV; Anna, Maci, and Kurt rode together in his car.

Kurt had doled out the three walkie-talkies he bought exclusively for the trip, mostly as a joke. But Anna noted that it would be good practice in downgrading from texting, because, she reminded everyone, this retreat would be inevitably low-tech. Maybe even no-tech.

"Breaker, breaker. This is Echo Delta checking in from location two. What's your twenty?" A crackle came over the radio as Eddie tested out his radio. Kurt had fallen behind the others at a red light.

"Come in, Eddie, this is Maci. We'll catch up once we hit the freeway," Maci replied into the yellow receiver. "So, should we play twenty questions or?" Maci continued.

"Nah, let's put on the radio. Do you have satellite, Kurt?" Anna cut her off.

"Um, of course. Have at it." He waved a hand toward the dials.

Anna made a move for the presets, browsing through a fantasy football channel, a tech news channel, headline news, another sports channel, and then two stations with electronic music.

"Shoulda guessed. Every single one of your presets is exactly what I would expect of you. Hah. Here, how about this," Anna twisted the dial until she came across an alternative rock station. She set the volume low so they could chat. The girls carried on a mundane conversation about work for a little while, which Kurt largely ignored, choosing instead to focus on the road.

After a slow hour, he finally broke back into the conversation. "Maci, will you radio the guys ahead and see if anyone needs to take a bathroom break? We are ahead of schedule, so we have the time," Kurt directed as he read the clock on the dashboard.

Anna interjected. "It's fine if we get in a little early. Knowing Mary, she was ready to go last night at the latest. She's probably waiting for us."

"Will she have other guests there perhaps checking out? We don't want to cause chaos," Kurt asked.

"Doubt it, but ya never know. Either way, we don't have to stop if we just wanna get up there," Anna replied.

"I'll check with the guys anyway," Maci chimed in. "Come in, Echo Dot whatever. Eddie? Alex? Are you both on?" Maci waited for the choppy responses.

"Alex here."

"Echo DELTA, Maci. It's Echo Delta. We're here. Come in? Over."

"Do you guys want to stop at the next rest area for a break?"

Maci released the radio button to ask Kurt where exactly the rest area was, but she was interrupted by the same question from Alex.

"Where's that? Over"

"Here, hand it to me," Kurt instructed Maci before turning down his car radio. "It's another half hour away, up the 101 farther and then off a little service exit. There's a gas station down the frontage road a few miles. It'll delay us by at least fifteen minutes to stop. Probably more. But we have the time. Over." Kurt answered.

"We won't need to, over." Alex returned.

"We can go either way," Eddie's voice cut in. "Rory had too much coffee, but he says that he can always pee out the window, worst case scenario." Anna and Maci giggled together, and Kurt couldn't tell if Eddie was joking. He stole a glance at Anna, who was still smiling broadly.

"Haha. Very funny. Just let me know in the next twenty minutes. We want to give Anna's sister a head's up if we plan to arrive much earlier than five." He let go of the radio button and peeked again at Anna, whose smile lingered. She shifted her attention to him.

"You know, Kurt, I am really starting to warm to the idea of your interest in my sister."

"What?" Maci practically shouted from the backseat. Kurt felt her grab his seat back and pull herself through the gap between his seat and Anna's. He cringed with irritation.

"Anna, with all due respect, this is a work trip. Your sister is beautiful, to be sure. But, again, I'm focusing on the team this weekend. Our needs. Not mine." He kept his gaze on the road and adjusted his hands on the steering wheel. It was one thing if something materialized between Mary and himself, but it was quite another if Anna *and* Maci got involved.

"Wait, what is going on? Anna? Are you setting them up?" Maci was desperate for any hint of drama or gossip. She thrived on it.

"Oh, absolutely not. No way on God's green earth would I ever set up any woman with any man. And there is definitely no way I'd set up my own sister. Come on, Maci. You should know me better than that by now." Anna turned her head toward her window before she finished. "Kurt thinks Mary is pretty, and Mary forced me to allow them to text each other ahead of this trip. That's all. I was just joking." Anna looked back at Kurt and broke back into a smile, waiting for his reaction. He had never seen a manipulative side of Anna, but he was now. *Why did she send him a second photo of Mary?*

"Oh my gosh, Kurt. I totally forgot you were single. And so is Anna's sister? Mary is her name? This is so exciting. It's like a little love field trip for you!" Maci squealed. Kurt couldn't help but glare into the rearview mirror at Maci.

"It's not a set-up, Maci. I'm going for FantasyCoin. That's it." He refocused on the road, his knuckles turning white as he gripped the wheel even harder.

"Well, I just mean that trips like this always result in hook-ups. It's the exact reason my boyfriend didn't want me to go at all," Maci giggled to herself, but Anna cut in.

"Maci, come on. It is a work event. I was making a lame joke. No hooking up. We all work together. And anyway, there will be literally only three women. Be cool." Anna flipped the sun visor down and opened the mirror to check her makeup.

"I know, I know," Maci backtracked. "I just mean, I think we are all looking for a chance to let loose. And, well, who knows what could happen?" With that, Kurt shifted uncomfortably in his seat and changed the subject.

"Anna, how was the report from the temp agency before we left? Did they have any final questions or concerns? Were the servers running smoothly?"

# Chapter 23

Mary had stationed herself on the leather armchair under the front window since she got Anna's text at half past four. They should arrive any moment, but she had grabbed her book beforehand to keep busy and distracted. She'd gotten as far as page three. Staring out the window consumed her.

Just before she got the text, she remembered that she once read that one of the rules of hospitality was to play background music. She pulled out her little CD player and tucked it on the shelf behind her reception desk. Then, she popped in a Christmas music album that Erica had given her years ago. She set it to play on loop.

Mary pulled out her phone to see if there was any update. When nothing appeared, she decided to busy herself away from the window. After all, she didn't want to look desperate.

So, she went to the back deck and grabbed her broom. She aimlessly swept at the miniature snow banks that had formed underneath the railings, until she heard the distinct crunch of tires on the front drive. She forced herself not to bounce in through the great room and head to the front door. She wanted the FantasyCoin people to believe she was busy.

She finished sweeping four or five errant pine needles from the edge of the deck when she heard the knocker pound against the front door. She tugged self-cautiously at her jeans and pulled her sweater back down in place before stepping in through the back door, crossing the great room and looking out the window, to see Anna' bright smile glowing at her from the front deck.

Mary picked up her pace until she was striding to the door. She opened it to a gush of fresh cold. Behind Anna was a line of seven others, shivering as they gripped overnight bags with bare hands.

"Anna! Everyone!" Mary beamed back at the group. "Please, come in! Welcome to Wood Smoke! Or I guess I should say welcome to

Maplewood! And your retreat!" She felt herself fumbling a bit, so she stepped back, holding the door wide. "Come in, come in!"

Anna stepped in first and gave her sister a big bear hug.

"Sis! I missed you! Let me introduce you to everyone. Come on guys, don't be shy!" Anna commanded the troop.

"This is Eddie. Here's Maci. That's Alex and Kato. Jace and Rory. Say hi, everyone!" Anna didn't wait for handshakes. Instead, she let the team awe over the vaulted, pine ceilings and massive stone fireplace while she pulled Mary back a step toward the door and toward the last person left to enter.

"Mare, this is my boss, Kurt Cutler. I know you two have sort of, well, chatted. But," Anna seemed to drop back and Kurt took a step over the threshold and into the lodge.

"Hi, Mary," his voice was deep but gentle. He put his hand out and Mary took it, overcome. He looked very different from the photo she'd found online the night before. He had the beginnings of a beard, and he was wearing something he could have pulled out of one of her brothers' closets. He looked nothing like the phony city hipster she'd seen hours earlier. She felt a push and tore her eyes away from Kurt's. Anna was nudging her.

"Mary? Hello?" Anna chuckled, but a glare crossed her face, catching Mary off-guard.

"Oh, I'm so sorry. Hi. I'm Mary, of course," she finally let his hand go as a small smile spread over her mouth. Anna grabbed her hand and pulled Mary over to the reception desk.

"Mary, why don't you check us in and then we can do a little tour?" Anna announced loudly so that the group could overhear. Kurt hung back at the door, letting the sisters huddle together.

Anna clutched Mary's shoulder, then whispered, "Snap out of it. He's not your type, anyway, trust me." Mary frowned back at Anna and pretended she didn't know what her sister was talking about.

"Okay, well, again. Welcome to Maplewood, everyone! Let me just start by getting each of your names, then I can pair you with a room number and key and we can get things going. How does that sound?" The group all mumbled in swift agreement, though a couple of them had started wandering into the great room.

# Chapter 24

Kurt left his hand on the doorknob to his guest room as he watched Mary, below. She smiled while she handed over a key to Eddie before glancing up in Kurt's direction, her smile spreading. He felt like a teenager again, but he smiled back down at her. Anna had taken it upon herself to navigate the moment when Mary had his room key ready, much to his irritation. But, he took it and moved upstairs immediately, needing to collect himself.

She was even lovelier in person than in either of the two pictures he had seen. He felt like he had won the lottery, but he wasn't sure if he could claim the prize. When she looked away again, he turned back to his door. A small iron stag hung next to the room number. Thinking it was a nice, rustic touch, he pressed his door open, stepped in, and pushed it closed.

Kurt took another three strides in and fell face first onto the bed, letting his duffel thump against the bed frame and onto the floor.

He flipped over, his hands on his chest, feeling his heart pumping. *Pull it together*, he reminded himself. It was still a work retreat. He promised Anna he would be respectful and appropriate and cool. But he was feeling amped.

The team could fend for themselves. He had to get to know Mary. He had to talk to her. Alone. Or, at least in a more intimate setting than the registration interaction had been.

He took three deep breaths in and out before pushing himself back up. Then, he stood and went to the small bathroom. Kurt took in the vintage fixtures and small claw foot tub. He was impressed. To buy one of those now - new or old - would be a serious financial investment he was certain.

He turned to look at himself in the medicine cabinet mirror that hung above the pedestal sink. His beard had seemingly filled in even more since his morning shower. He considered adding a splash of cologne, but couldn't remember if he'd packed it.

He paced back out to his duffel and hauled it up onto the bed. There he found his toiletries bag. He stuck his hand inside, clawing around before he finally dumped the contents onto the bag. No cologne. Not even aftershave. At least he had his deodorant. He returned to the bathroom to splash his face with cold water. After that, he went ahead and brushed his teeth, for good measure.

After one last preview in the little mirror, he went back to the room to pull out his clothes and hang any shirts. It was then that he realized how quaint the room was. It felt like a miniature cabin all on its own.

The pinewood walls captured the rustic element that over-the-top home renovation shows tried so hard to execute. He needed to be sure to compliment Mary on the Lodge. She really nailed it.

Anna had Kurt thinking the experience would be far less impressive than the Lodge and its property actually were. This place really was a terrific investment on Mary's part.

He felt his pulse pick up again as he thought of her. He quickly checked his watch to see he had been hiding out for nearly fifteen minutes. He quickly pulled his shirts out of his bag and laid them out before leaving the room and heading back downstairs.

As he hit the top landing of the staircase, he saw that the others weren't by the reception desk or in the great room. As he trotted down the steps, he had a view to the dining room. They weren't there or in the kitchen.

Finally, as he made his way into the great room he saw them through the wooden French doors at the back of the room. They were huddled on the deck, facing Mary who was animatedly explaining something. He caught her eye as she let her hands lilt to her sides and she paused in her speech. In one synchronized sweep, the group twisted their heads back to see what Mary was looking at it.

He first caught Anna's reaction: an eye roll. Then Eddie's: a goofy hang-ten sign. Then he noticed Maci break into a knowing smile while Jace waved. Kurt felt awkward that he hadn't joined them to begin with. He didn't want to come across as disconnected, so he hurriedly crossed the room and shrugged his way through the door that Kato held open for him.

"*There* you are, Kurt," Rory called from the far side of the deck. He could have sworn he heard one of them snicker.

"I am so sorry everyone. I'm so sorry, Mary," he said as he locked eyes with her. "I completely got carried away admiring the accommodations upstairs. This place is great. Nothing like you described, Anna," he said pointedly in her direction. Stealing a glance at her, he saw her frown and cross her arms in a pout. Mary looked to her also. Anna shrugged.

"Thanks, Kurt." She then looked at Anna. "And Anna, thank you for suggesting that you host your retreat here." Mary smirked at her sister before going on. "Okay, well, I guess that concludes the run-down on our scheduled activities. As you can tell, I'm encouraging ample downtime. My hope is that you will all enjoy this as a vacation as much as a work thing. And I think Anna told you, but the lodge has no Internet and very limited cell service." Mary finished her spiel with a nod to her sister. She clasped her hands and smiled at the group.

Kurt gauged the others' reactions; they were murmuring and smiling and seemed genuinely happy. No one even so much as muttered a complaint about the "no Internet, limited service" bit.

"So, Mary, can we check out our rooms now that the tour is over?" Anna jumped in.

"Of course! Head on up, everyone. Dinner will be served at six o'clock, so you have…" Mary paused to reference her slim leather wrist watch, "About an hour. Make yourselves at home! Oh, and one more thing. The property sits on over 20 acres. You are more than welcome to roam in the woods. But consider leaving a trail of breadcrumbs, just in case." And then, like a little old man with a secret, she winked at them.

With that, Kurt fell in love.

# Chapter 25

The others had already walked in, and it was just Kurt, Anna, and Mary left on the deck. As Kurt turned to follow them in, Mary strode toward him and reached her hand up to tap his shoulder.

"Kurt, hang on a sec."

She could feel the taut muscles under his cotton shirt. It caught her off-guard. She could feel Anna's eyes burning into the back of her head, but she didn't care.

Mary considered her prior notions about the weekend. 1. Kurt was too much of a pretty boy to be attractive. 2. It would be silly to pin any hopes on making some sort of love connection with her sister's boss. 3. This weekend was a business transaction and little else. All of it had flown out the window when Kurt stepped across the threshold and into the lodge.

Sure, Mary had been attracted to men before. But nothing so far, *nothing*, had felt like *this*. But, Mary was smart. Smart enough to play it a little cool and smart enough to be a professional.

Mary gestured to Anna, who would be sharing her room since the Lodge only offered seven guest rooms. "Anna, why don't you go get unpacked in my room. I'm going to take Kurt on the little tour he missed," she directed, feeling bold. Anna's mouth dropped open, and Kurt's eyebrows shot up in question.

"Are you sure? I would think he could figure things out on his own," Anna pursed her lips.

Kurt shoved his hands snugly into his jean pockets. "Actually, a tour would be wonderful. I'd love to hear more about this place."

Anna's hands flew up. "Fine. You two *behave*," She snorted as she tugged open the door and shuffled inside. Mary's cheeks grew hot and she looked down. Kurt cleared his throat. His discomfort was palpable, which made Mary even more upset with her sister's inappropriate behavior. She had to speak up.

"Um, I am so sorry. Anna is... well..." Mary didn't know how to finish the sentence without throwing her sister under the bus. "She's my sister, I guess," she laughed, awkwardly.

"I totally get it. I see Anna in the office and at work events all the time. She is fierce. She's focused on her career and making it, and there's a lot to respect about that. She's certainly a successful woman. Professionally," he added. Mary considered this for a moment before redirecting the conversation.

"Anna really is great, but we will take her with a grain of salt for the weekend. I'd love to show you the property so you can see what you're paying for."

She started Kurt's tour by explaining the nightly bonfire plans and the news that they would be having chili for dinner with freshly baked rolls and sweet tea. His mouth seemed to water at that, giving Mary another boon.

From there, she turned it on even further, sweeping him into the kitchen and dining room, explaining the history of the lodge and her own acquisition of it. He was a great listener and complimented just about everything she pointed out, from the farmhouse table to the original stone fireplace.

They finished at the hot cocoa station, where Mary insisted on mixing Kurt a mug and adding in marshmallows and peppermint bark. He sipped at it gingerly while they sat together on the love seat.

The others were still upstairs, except for Maci, who was trying desperately to find a hole in the wooded canopy for cell service. The snow had stopped, and she was frantic to text her boyfriend and let him know she'd made it, safe and sound.

Kurt and Mary laughed together as they watched Maci flounder around in the fluffy snow without snow boots.

"Hmm," Mary thought aloud. "Maybe I ought to go save her from herself and offer her a pair of my old boots."

Kurt leaned in towards Mary a bit to get a better view of Maci.

"That would be generous of you. I promise I sent out a group email reminding everyone of the conditions. I'd hate to have you think I dropped the ball.

"Oh, don't worry about it. I am used to having guests from the valley who come ill-equipped for the weather. It's understandable. How can the weather be so wildly different when you don't even leave the state?" Mary rose up from the sofa to go get the boots.

Kurt quickly stood, too, waiting for her to return. She crossed to the entryway closet. When she got there, she flipped on the light switch and saw that she had stowed her box of extras on the shelf. She had a vague recollection of taking pains to drag her step ladder from the shed in order to store it all *last* season. She sighed as she tested her reach. Not even close.

Kurt all but bounded over. "Here, I can help," he said as he waited for Mary to move aside. She thanked him and watched as his lithe body plucked the box off the shelf in one fluid motion. The thin fabric of his shirt showed off his lean and defined body. She felt a twinge of exhilaration and stepped back a little farther so he could swing the box down between them.

"Where to?" He asked, looking at her earnestly, as though this was the most important job of the day.

"Let's just take it to the back door and keep it there for now. Might come in handy for someone else. I have a little bit of everything in there. Mostly brand new stuff that I thought to have on hand."

She followed him as he took the box to the floor by the back door. She bent over to pull the boots and could feel Kurt's eyes on her. Smiling to herself, Mary lingered for a moment before rising and opening the door.

"Maci!" Mary called out into the snowy woods.

"Yeah?" Came the young woman's voice from somewhere beyond the fire pit. "Trying to find a signal; be right there!" She yelled back.

"I have a pair of boots for you! I'll leave them by the door here!" Mary replied.

Kurt held the door open for Mary as she stepped back inside. Once they both brushed off the chill, they saw the others tracking down the staircase behind Anna, who looked like she had cooled off.

"We're starving. Can we eat a little earlier?" Anna spoke on behalf of the group.

"Absolutely. Come on into the dining room, everyone. I'll get things started."

"Need any help?" Kurt offered.

"Oh, sure," Mary smiled up at him before she directed Anna to set out the plates and mason jars.

"Around here, you'll be put to work if you don't stay out of the way," Anna joked to the team. "Come help me, Eddie," she instructed, keeping an eye on Kurt.

As they got the table set, Mary and Kurt went into the kitchen. She had him carry to the dining table a serving bowl of salad and a little dish filled with ranch dressing. As he did, she stuck the rolls into the oven and went to the crockpot to stir the chili. When she lifted the steam-soaked lid, a hot fragrance escaped and trickled through the air and into the rest of the lodge.

It smelled like company, as her mom would say. Mary smiled to herself and repositioned the lid.

"Smells amazing in here!" It was Maci, who had found her way in, shoes nowhere to be seen. Mary looked down at the girl's wet socks and laughed. "I am so sorry, Mary. I know. Totally gross. I'll go up and change. I just wanted to thank you for the boots. I should have packed better, but I'll definitely use them next time I go out there."

"If you need a fresh pair of socks, I have those, too, Mary squeezed Maci's shoulder.

Maci reciprocated with a broad smile and trotted up the stairs as she called behind, "I've got a pair, no worries!"

"Oh, Maci," Mary stopped her. "Since you're on your way past the reception, can you start the music back up? It's behind the desk." Mary wanted to be sure to have Christmas music in the background of their dinner.

Kurt swept back into the kitchen and Mary felt like the whole day had been orchestrated. She had a familiar feeling with Kurt, and she wasn't the sort to keep that kind of thing buried in her heart.

# Chapter 26

The scent that radiated out from the kitchen almost knocked Kurt backward as he set the salad and dressing down on the table.

The others were talking shop, but Kurt was too focused. He couldn't believe how easy it was to talk with Mary and be in her presence. When he first saw her as he walked through the front door, he couldn't fathom feeling comfortable around her. Something about her was enigmatic and hard to read.

But slowly, as she took him from the deck to inside and around the lodge, they settled in together. Most of the conversation had been small talk, and he enjoyed hearing about the history of the place. But each time they made eye contact, his heart raced again. He thought the same thing was happening with Mary.

He had to address it, but he didn't know how or when, especially with Anna so clearly against his growing crush. He couldn't count on having more alone time with Mary, so he dipped back into the kitchen while Anna continued telling the group about how she helped Mary decorate the Lodge.

As he walked back into the kitchen, Mary twirled around from the counter, facing him squarely.

"Kurt, hi," she said. Kurt thought he detected a flush to her cheeks. Or maybe it was the subtle makeup she was wearing. He couldn't tell if she was actually wearing any, and he loved that. Her natural look was overwhelmingly attractive to him.

"Mary, hi," he grinned and moved closer to her. She peeked behind him.

"The salad is out there and it looks like we have some time before the main course," he met her gaze.

"Yes, thank you." She glanced again behind him, almost nervously.

"Is everything okay?" He asked, searching her expression as he scratched his jawline. As if in response, she tucked a strand of hair behind her ear. It drove him wild.

"Yes, I just wanted to tell you," she started. He contemplated moving closer but decided not to risk making her uncomfortable. So he waited until she found her words.

She stole one more glance behind him then peeked over at the oven before continuing. "I wanted to say that, I'm really enjoying your company. I'm so glad you booked the weekend here. I," she hesitated. "I just feel," She stopped again, darting her eyes everywhere but at him.

"Mary, I know I told Anna I would play it cool, but I have to interrupt you," he broke in. She finally looked into his eyes. "This lodge is incredible. And you... You're also... well, I guess I just mean that I agree. I am really enjoying your company, too. And your place is. It's really great," he smiled down at her, feeling a rush inside his chest, but her tentative smile fell a bit, and he could tell instantly that he missed the mark.

Mary turned away. "That's so great," she replied as she busied herself by rinsing a ladle in the sink. "I'm glad we are all off to a good start. I hope to offer your team exactly what you expected." She then turned back, abruptly, and flushed, her mouth downturned. He took a step back.

"Mary," he started. But she turned again to the sink.

"Can you tell the others that I'll be out with the rolls in two minutes sharp?" She asked as she continued facing the other way.

"Oh, sure," he tried to soften his voice as much as he could. But he had ruined the moment, somehow.

Crushed and confused, he ducked out of the kitchen and back to the dining room, where the rest of the crew sat rapt listening now to Eddie deliver a long-winded joke. Kurt found an empty spot on the end, next to Kato, and slumped down into it. Maci returned from upstairs with her fresh socks on and phone still glued to her hand.

The rest of dinner went about the same. Mary asked Anna to help her as she served the table of hungry travelers, and she let Anna pour Kurt's tea and pass him the rolls.

Mary informed the group that she would excuse herself, allowing them to bond over dinner without her interference. Anna protested, and Kurt began to as well, but Mary put her hand up and firmly directed them to enjoy the meal and each other's company. She would get the main course ready and bring it out shortly.

Kurt sighed and was only able to swallow down a couple bites of the delicious home-cooked meal. He had lost his appetite and his enthusiasm.

But he wasn't going to lose a chance at this girl.

# Chapter 27

Mary looked over her shoulder toward the dining room. Had she misread him? Was Anna wrong when she said Kurt had a crush on her? She couldn't understand why he would interrupt her confession to compliment the Lodge, of all things. Sure, she appreciated it, but she was clearly taking the conversation in a different direction. He either didn't get it or didn't want to hear it. She could kick herself for not being better at flirting. But, then, maybe he was saving her embarrassment. Maybe he was trying to be professional.

Mary took a small scoop of the chili from the pot and tested it. It was deliciously perfect- just the right balance of savory and spicy. Still disappointed and confused, she realized she had to move on and keep up appearances. Just as she grabbed for her worn red oven mitt, the timer went off on the rolls. She opened the oven door and stuck her mitt-covered hand into the warm chamber and slid the tray of fresh rolls out.

After setting the rolls on the kitchen island, she crossed to the fridge and pulled out the tub of butter she'd made a couple weeks back. After a few moments of churning the butter to soften it, she scooped a dollop into the crest of each roll.

Then, she brought her bread basket to the island and lined the bottom with a green tea towel. She carefully transferred each roll into the basket and tucked a second towel over it. She started to feel like she just wanted to crawl in a corner and munch away at a warm, buttery roll. She knew she might be acting a little sensitive, but she didn't have enough practice in navigating crushes. The last time she actually had a true crush was probably high school.

Maybe, Mary thought, as she moved back to the crockpot, she misread Kurt entirely. Maybe she just needed to be herself and see where that would take her after all. And with that, she grabbed two dish towels to lift the pot of chili out of the base and marched directly into the dining room.

Everyone was happily sipping away at their sweet tea. But when she passed behind the bench to the buffet to set the chili down, she caught Kurt's eyes on her from the far end of the table. Mary tried to avoid looking back, but she felt herself grow hot. She realized it would be too cramped for the guests to serve themselves, so she announced that she would ladle the chili into their bowls. Thankfully, Anna piped up.

"I'll help, Mary. I can pass out bowls." Anna jumped out of her seat and grabbed the bowls, efficiently passing one stack to Eddie to pass along his bench and one stack to Maci to pass along hers.

As Anna conducted the place settings, Mary glimpsed Kurt, who was still watching her. They locked eyes and she felt butterflies brush up through her insides. Kurt offered her a small smile, his eyebrows knitting up together. Mary could read hope in his expression and her embarrassment melted away. She smiled back with her whole face, but anything more would have to wait for later.

She never made a habit of dining with guests, no matter how familiar. Before she returned to the kitchen to start tidying up, she picked up the chili pot and started heaping servings into each bowl.

Eddie, Kato, and Rory all thanked her as she went, taking care not to dribble between ladles. Anna passed on the chili and decided to stick with salad and a roll since she had gone vegetarian for the month.

Mary then squeezed her way back to the head of the table to start on the second row. She ladled chili into the bowl of cute little Maci, who had changed into her pajamas.

"Thank you so much, Mary! I feel like I'm at my grandma's house for Christmas. This has been such an adorable day. I can't even stand it," Maci gushed like a teenager. Surprisingly it didn't annoy Mary. Instead, it endeared Maci to her.

"That is the highest compliment, I would say," Mary replied with a warm smile.

Mary carried on, wedging her way between the wall and the bench. She served Jace next and then Alex. Finally, she made her way to the very end, where Kurt sat, waiting. He had let his gaze drift out of the bay window, at the glow of the falling snow.

Crammed behind him, she couldn't avoid brushing his shoulder with her chest as she leaned slightly over him to scoop chili into his bowl. She noticed him tense up.

"Thank you, Mary," he turned and looked up at her once she drew the ladle back.

"Mmhmm," she murmured. She had to avoid making eye contact or else she would break into a full blush in front of everyone. And, although she didn't really mind if anyone knew she had a crush, she still wanted to remain generally professional. As she began to squeeze her slight frame back behind the bench, the team returned to their conversation.

Once she made her way to the threshold of the kitchen, she instinctively turned back to survey the scene. When she did, she saw that Kurt had been following her with his eyes the whole time.

Her eyes then flit to Anna, who was glaring at her, arms crossed, jaw set.

Warmth spread up to her face as her heart pounded. She smiled, tightly, and whipped back around, unable to stand the tension.

A moment later, she had dumped the leftovers into a storage container and then rested the crockpot in the deep industrial sink and filled it with hot water. She squeezed some dish soap into her sponge when she heard someone walk into the kitchen.

Assuming it had to be Anna coming to chastise Mary for the obvious way she was acting around Kurt, she carried on scrubbing the pot began to talk without turning around.

"What can I say, Ann? He's insanely hot. In fact, how have *you* resisted this whole time you've been working with him?" When Anna didn't respond right away, Mary froze. After another beat, she whipped around. It wasn't Anna.

# Chapter 28

Kurt was stunned. After initially worrying that he had ruined his chance, he finally figured out his error. So, here he was, back in the kitchen to talk to Mary privately and let her know just how impressed he was with *her*, not the lodge.

He practically melted into the floor hearing what he did.

Shocked and uncertain of how to respond, he just waited for her to turn around. When she did and they looked at each other, his heart began to pound.

Her hair had gotten a little wilder, somehow, in the last ten minutes. Her face was flushed, and her mouth was parted open in surprise.

"I, um..." they spoke at once, their words colliding.

"Mary..."

Mary looked beyond him and into the dining room. Kurt cleared his voice.

"Listen, Kurt," Mary continued, deeming the situation safe. "That was super embarrassing. Wow." She stopped abruptly, her eyes trained on a spot over his shoulder.

Just as Kurt opened his mouth to assure her that the feeling was absolutely mutual, Anna brushed in behind him and toward the sink.

"I ended up breaking my promise to myself and tasting Kato's dang chili. I dropped it right onto my top. Ugh," she spat as she splashed water onto the front of the blue cotton sweater.

Mary shifted her weight before interjecting, "I have to go. Kurt, if there was a question you had, I'm sure Anna can answer it." Her embarrassment was palpable as she suddenly spun out of the kitchen and headed toward the staircase.

Anna's eyes were trained on Kurt as he watched Mary leave.

"What happened?" she asked, pressing a dry dish towel to the chili stain. She was all but seething, having some idea of what was about to transpire.

"Nothing, Anna," Kurt muttered and turned back to the dining table.

"Great. I told you to back off," Anna called after him as she left to follow Mary upstairs. Kurt quickly looked at the others at the table to see if they had overheard the commotion.

Fortunately, the guys were laughing at Eddie, who was describing something animatedly. Maci, however, was quietly observing him as she gnawed on a roll.

"Hey Mace," Kurt said to her as he started to sit to her left. "Can you slide down so I can fit here?" He asked gently. She pushed her way over, keeping her head crooked in his direction.

"How's the love connection going?" She asked between bites.

"There's no love connection, Maci." Kurt couldn't help but laugh in spite of himself. One of the reasons he hired Maci was because she was fun, and he thought she would help the rest of the team to lighten up sometimes. It turned out that Eddie was the class clown of the group, but Maci was still a breath of fresh air. She often said what was on her mind, but she did it with cheer, somehow.

"Yes, there is." Maci turned back to scrolling through old photos on her phone. Kurt studied her, waiting for an elaboration. When none came, he had no choice but to give himself up.

"What do you mean?" He asked, perking back up a bit. Maci kept scrolling, uncharacteristically oblivious to his renewed interest.

"I mean she's obviously interested in you," she replied as she set her phone down to take a sip of her sweet tea. "She has to be professional. She's running our so-called retreat, Kurt. What do you expect? Her to fawn over you?" Maci finished her drink and looked up at him. "I promise you. She is as into you as a girl can possibly be. The difference between her approach and yours is that she doesn't know the rest of us. She thinks she has to act a little cool."

"So, she's playing hard to get?" Kurt propped his elbow up on the table and settled his head into his hand. He gave Maci a weary look.

"No. No. No." Maci adjusted her position in order to face him. "I don't think she's playing a game at all." Maci shook her head and her short hair fanned out, making her look like a little fairy. Kurt stifled a laugh before his face fell back into a frown.

"I'm getting mixed signals, though."

"Yeah, I see that. I think it is a little complicated for her. Anna is obviously protective, although I don't know if it's Mary she is protecting, or if it's *you*." At that, Kurt's eyebrows shot up.

"Protecting *me*?" He asked, again confused. He realized his relationship with Brittany, though troubled, never seemed to carry intricacies like this.

Their communication was always to the point and never held implication or innuendo. As he thought about it, he also realized that maybe *that* was the problem. A distinct lack of innuendo.

Maci looked back at the guys, who were starting to get up and clear their places, still largely ignorant of Kurt and Maci's private conversation. She returned her attention to Kurt and said, "Yeah. In fact, I think Anna is maybe even a little…" she paused for effect.

"What?" Kurt prompted her, impatiently. "Angry? Concerned? What?"

"Jealous," Maci replied, pointedly.

# Chapter 29

As soon as Mary sank onto her bed, head in hands, a rap sounded at her door. She felt a headache coming on. Too little caffeine. Too many emotions.

How ridiculous.

She was falling for her sister's boss: a man she had never met. A man who lived in a different city- a big city. A man who was her guest. And, to top it all off, she had started to admit this to him only for him to interrupt her and compliment the stupid Lodge, instead.

She fell back on the bed, her hair splaying around her, arms crossed over her face to dull the daylight streaking in from the bedside window.

Another set of sharp percussions cut into Mary's attempt to ignore her problems. A voice followed.

"Mary, open the door, it's me," Anna demanded from the other side.

*Ugh.* Mary thought. She peeked out from her arm before rolling off the bed to the door. Without bothering to check through the peep-hole, she pulled the door open and flopped her way back to the bed, where she returned to her previous position.

"You have a key," she snorted as she threw her arms back over her face.

"What is going on?" Anna retorted, falling onto the bed beside her sister. "What happened with Kurt? I told you men are scum. It's obvious you're into him, Mary. And, frankly, it's a little stupid. You could do way better. If you just came to the valley with me for a weekend, then we could go out to the clubs, party, meet a million guys. And no commitment. You don't have to get sucked into some disappointing relationship with someone who fooled you into believing he loved you." Anna seemed to have more to say, but Mary sat up abruptly and cut her off.

"Enough, Anna. Enough of the man-bashing. Enough of the one-night-stand crap. Enough of trying to turn me into you." Mary stood, crossing her arms over her chest and shifting her weight to her right hip.

She stared down at her older sister, who looked like a deer in headlights at the sudden accusations.

Mary gave her a minute to respond, and when Anna just sat there, eyes wide, Mary continued. "You are clearly unhappy with something that has happened in your life. Maybe, in fact, you are unhappy with how it's going right now. But you're barking up the wrong tree. Maybe I'm not going to be the perfect little housewife like Erica, but I'm not going to head in your extreme, either. Sure, I agree with you. I need to get out more. I need to meet more people. In fact, actually, I would be happy to meet someone who made me feel the way that your boss is freaking making me feel!" Mary's voice rose and her arms came down to her sides in fists. "I don't want your life, Anna, but I *do* want *your* boss. There. I said it. Okay?"

Anna's jaw set and her eyes narrowed. Mary turned away from her and fiddled with a knob on the dresser behind her.

"*Who are you?*" Anna hissed as she stood and crossed to Mary's back. "What happened to your priorities? The Lodge? Being independent and making your own way in this world? You have one hot guy turn up at your door and you let all that fall away so that you can pursue your basic instincts. You call my behavior indecent, but look at you."

Mary snapped around, fire rising inside her.

"One hot guy? Is that what this is all about? Do *you* like Kurt?" Mary's eyes blazed at her sister, realizing for the first time why Anna had acted so righteous.

Anna blinked, briefly, mouth opening to respond. Mary didn't let her. "You are jealous, Anna. And you have no idea how to deal with it. You have liked Kurt. Maybe more than the guys you meet at clubs. And now, he likes someone else. But that someone is me. And you lost. For the first time, maybe. You lost. Your younger country-bumpkin sister with a failing business likes the same guy as you, and he might like her back." Mary was done.

"Wrong. I don't like Kurt, I... I" Anna stuttered over her words, shifting her gaze toward the door before settling it on the floor in front her feet. She rubbed one booted foot over the other, silently. Finally, she finished her sentence. "I mean... yeah. I have always thought Kurt was attractive. But I'm serious that I'm really not interested in him, Mare,"

Anna looked back up, earnestly searching Mary's eyes, pleading her sister to believe her.

Mary's face softened and she relaxed her hands at her sides.

"Anna, I don't even think he is interested. That's the reason I ran up here in the first place. Well, part of the reason. First of all, I am trying very hard to be professional in front of your staff members. I hope that is coming across?"

Anna nodded her head, urging Mary to continue.

"And second of all, I just made a fool out of myself in front of him." Mary waited for something, anything from her big sister. Validation. Affirmation. A vote of confidence for once.

Anna seemed to carefully weigh her response. "I'm sure he thinks you're pretty, Mare. I mean, you *are* pretty," she stopped.

Mary could tell more was coming, though.

"Mary, you cannot date Kurt. He's my boss and this is a business weekend. I'm sorry," Anna's face set, "I'm not supporting you." As she finished her sentence, a tear fell from her eye. She brushed it away as quickly as it fell and again crossed her arms.

Mary felt like she had been slapped in the face. Anna put her in a difficult position. She had to act like the innkeeper, the one in charge of the Wood Smoke Lodge. But infatuation was still creeping in.

Anna interjected, "I'm gonna use your bathroom. We'll pretend that this never happened. No crush. No sister fight. Okay? Be right out, then we can start fresh?" Anna walked away without waiting for a reply.

And it was that small, dismissive act that helped Mary make up her mind. She opened the door of her room and left.

She needed to go find Kurt.

# Chapter 30

Kurt wasn't dumb. He realized that Mary rushed out because Anna came into the kitchen. He was starting to be annoyed with Anna. Once she, too, left, he figured he'd wait for Mary and pitch in at the table.

The others were done clearing their plates. Kato and Maci went to the hot cocoa bar and mixed themselves a couple mugs. Eddie, Rory, Alex, and Jace were walking out onto the back deck. He remembered Jace talking about bringing cigars for everyone and figured that was their plan.

He grabbed his bowl and bread plate, cleared them into the trash, and then took his glass from the table to the sink and rinsed it. He opened the dishwasher and quickly loaded his dishes and the others' before drying his hands on one of the stacks of crisp green dish towels. He folded the towel back up and placed it on the edge of the sink.

He expected either Anna or Mary to return in that time, but when they hadn't, he thought he would join the others out on the back deck.

As he opened the back door, the scent of rich cigar smoke swirled around the cold night air, drawing him out. The snow had stopped. The guys had a nice little fire blazing in the pit.

"Boss!" Eddie cheered for him. He had never met anyone as upbeat and happy as Eddie always seemed to be.

"Eddie, my man," Kurt replied, a sadness in his voice. He moved down the steps and to the circle of wooden stumps, crossing behind Eddie, who looked to be wearing about five sweatshirts. Kurt squeezed Eddie's shoulders through the thick stack of fabric and then sank onto the stump between Eddie and Jace, who was puffing away.

"Light me up, Jace," Kurt said. Jace obliged excitedly, going into a long overview of the origins of the cigar brand and how he managed to acquire them. Kurt nodded along while the guys digressed into more work talk. They mostly analyzed other cryptocurrencies and bemoaned the inevitable market downturn.

Slowly, Kurt faded out from listening and happened to see a flash in the glass of the French door behind them. He craned his neck forward and noticed Anna's back against the door. He scratched his beard and wondered what Mary and Anna talked about.

Was Maci right? When Kurt thought back over the last couple days of texts and the awkward conversation he had with Anna in his office, it seemed plausible.

He had never thought about Anna that way. She was a nice-looking girl, but not his type. A party girl wasn't his type. He was low key. He wanted a laid-back life. He saw a future for himself of quiet nights at home, helping his kids with homework while his wife baked cookies. Anna had never been part of that picture, and she never would be.

Mary, however, fit the image perfectly.

Kurt was dying to have another chance at speaking with Mary in private, but he didn't want to make her uncomfortable again. And, he didn't want to upset Anna. Despite his irritation, she was his Vice President and he valued her as an employee. He couldn't afford to have a rift with her, especially right now.

He kept his eye on the window of the door, waiting for Anna to move or to come out- anything that would give him a clue about Mary's movements.

"Kurt!" Kato jolted him out of his focus. "Kurt? Your turn!" Kurt looked at Kato and then the others. He had completely missed the conversation.

"Huh?" He asked, suddenly feeling worn out.

"Who's on your *list?*" Jace pressed him, with a knowing look.

"What list?" Kurt asked, glancing back at the door. Anna's back was still to it, but he could tell she was talking to someone. Her hands kept coming up and down in front of her and to the side.

"You know. The *list*. Who you'd date in the office. Except, we're extending ours to the office building since, well, two women is too few to work with.

Kurt had kept his eyes on the door and saw Anna leave the window frame. He stood.

"None of them," he said as he stood and absently handed his cigar to Jace. "Here, hold this for me."

"Hey, it's just for fun, Kurt," Jace took the cigar and looked up at his boss, ashamedly.

"Yeah, we're not being serious, just in good fun," Eddie chimed in. Kurt was already to the door when he realized how he'd sounded.

"No. Don't worry about it, guys. Go for it. Have all the fun you want. I need to see to some business," Kurt finished and stepped inside. As he did, he thought he caught one of them say something about Anna. He didn't care.

Once in, he caught Mary and Maci step around the corner into the kitchen. Anna was heading up the stairs. Maci was now too involved. He'd embarrass himself if he confronted Mary with Maci around.

He checked his watch to see that it was past seven. He felt tired enough to pass out and contemplated heading upstairs. Before that, he wanted to linger a little bit and give Mary a chance to see that he was available. He thought about conversation starters. Maybe he'd ask what was in store for their activities tomorrow? No. Then she'd think he was still too focused on the Lodge and her business.

He walked over to the hot cocoa table and poured hot water from the insulated pitcher into one of the wide-mouthed blue mugs. He scooped some cocoa into the mug and grabbed a peppermint bark straw to stir. He gave it a minute, his eye on the general vicinity of the kitchen, before sipping the hot drink. Though he was still tempted to go up to his room and crash out, he decided instead to set up camp in the living room.

He picked a spot on the long, overstuffed leather sofa that faced the kitchen and dining room and pulled out his phone to browse. As soon as he clicked it to life, he saw that he had 47 new emails. But, when he tried to open his email app, all he got was the loading symbol and a blank screen.

No service. He had forgotten. Having no interest in wandering around the snowy woods in the pitch black, he folded himself farther into the pillows on the sofa and sipped at the warm cocoa. He scanned the room for magazines or books and saw a short stack on the floor under the coffee table. He bent down beneath the table to reach for one of the books when he saw feet move out from the kitchen to the dining room.

# Chapter 31

"Ow!" Mary heard a deep, loud cry from the living room as she and Maci went to set the table for breakfast.

She snapped her head and saw a hand run over thick, dark hair. It was Kurt, wincing from hitting his head on the underside of the coffee table, apparently.

"Are you okay?" She strode around the protrusion of the fireplace and toward him, leaving Maci behind her.

"Yeah, ouch. What is that table made of?" He asked as he rubbed his head and leaned back onto the sofa, his eyes shifting from the table to her.

"Iron. Wrought iron frame. At least, that's what my dad said. Are you sure you're okay? Do you need ice?" She asked as she neared him. He steadied his gaze and let his hand drop. A smile crept across his face.

"I'm better now," he replied, shyly. "But I was hoping to talk to you." Now it was Kurt's turn to look past Mary and into the dining room. She turned her head back to see Maci watching them, phone in one hand, still. Mary wondered what Maci could be doing with a service-less phone.

"I'm going now," Maci tucked her phone in her back pocket and padded past them, through the door, and out onto the back deck.

They watched as she slid her feet into the boots Mary had loaned her and then picked her way down the icy steps and to the fire pit. They could hear the boys' raucous voices die down as she approached. Kurt chuckled.

"What?" Mary asked, confused. As she watched him respond, she slowly dipped down onto the sofa next to him. He didn't move.

"Oh, nothing," he started as he stared out through the glass doors. He looked back at her, smiling. "Well, the guys were talking about their 'work list.'" He made air quotes with his long fingers.

"'Work list?'" Mary pantomimed back. "What's that?"

"Well, it's like a list of who you…" he paused, glancing down at his lap. Mary thought she detected a hint of color rise in the hollows beneath his cheekbones. She caught on.

"*Want?*" She finished for him. His head jolted back up and they locked eyes.

"Something like that," he sputtered. "But don't worry. They are all nerds. Respectful ones. They mean no harm, trust me. I'm one of them." One side of his mouth turned up in a half grin. He looked like a mischievous frat boy, and Mary felt a little uneasy.

"One of them, huh? So, who is on your list then? It's gotta be either Maci or Anna, right?" She all but snapped. She couldn't help it. She was typically a very even-keeled person. But today she had felt hot and cold and all over the place.

"As I told the guys before I came in here to find you, no one from work is on any list of mine. My interests are elsewhere." As he said this, Mary felt her heart pound and her senses sharpen. She could smell the cold winter air, heavy with a mix of wood smoke and cigar smoke. She could feel the warm glow of the embers from the fire that was starting to tucker out. She could taste remnants from the peppermint bark she'd been sucking on as she'd asked Maci to help set the table. And, when he pushed his hand down on the sofa to turn to face her, Mary felt the tips of Kurt's fingers brush against hers. She tensed but left her hand there. His stayed too. She stared down at the space between them, paralyzed by the suspense.

"Where would that be?" She asked, and her gaze crawled back up his torso and past his neck into his probing stare. She saw dark eyelashes, framing clear irises. His full lips, peeking out from his beard.

"Right here," he answered and covered her hand with his. Her chest rose and fell over and again, and her back arched slightly as she laced her fingers up and through his. She glanced over his shoulder and out the glass at the others. They were beginning to huddle together closer to the fire.

"What's going on?" Anna's voice fell down upon them from the landing overhead.

# Chapter 32

Mary's head snapped up at her sister. Kurt's too. He felt Mary slip her hand back out from his, and his heart sank. He tucked his own hand into his lap.

Mary spoke up.

"Ann," she started. But she didn't get a chance.

"So much for a professional retreat. Looks like neither of you cares to follow through on your promises." Anna's voice was thick with anger. Kurt could tell that whatever their earlier conversation included, it didn't end well.

"I didn't promise you anything, Anna." Mary stood and faced her sister.

"Whatever. I'm going out to the fire pit. You two enjoy yourselves."

Anna didn't so much as look at them as she passed by and out the doors onto the deck. Kurt watched her wrap her arms around herself and wobble her way down the steps.

"Kurt, I'm so sorry about my sister. I hope none of this is making you think less of her. She respects you a lot, as her boss. She cares about her job very much. I think," Mary paused. She seemed to be considering something. "I think this is awkward for her. Our... well... whatever this is," Mary waved her hand back and forth between them.

"I can see that. And she has a point. Maybe it's not appropriate for me to hit on the owner of our retreat." He smiled wryly.

"Oh, no. That part is very appropriate, for *you*. Less so, however, for *me*, as strange as that may sound." Mary added, "What's inappropriate for you is that you are coming on to someone in front of your subordinates."

"Anna is the only one who minds. Remember, the work list? Yeah, these guys need all the examples they can get." Kurt hesitated before he went on to explain. "Here's the thing, Mary."

She sat back down, a look of worry crossing her face.

"We are on a trip as a group of people who work together. But I made it extraordinarily clear to everyone that this was a social, laid-back, fun trip. They can throw back beers. They can smoke cigars until their lungs turn black. They can talk about girls they like. Maci can gush over her boyfriend and glue herself to her phone or do whatever she wants to do. *Anna* has been the one who has been skeptical of this. She is trying to keep things clean for us. But, let's get real. We are a very small and very unique business. And while we do answer to a board of supervisors, we don't have an HR person. We only really need to worry about our personal or professional conduct if it actually crosses a legal line."

Mary held her hand up. "What about morality? Ethics?"

Kurt tilted his head up and considered this, before responding. "Mary, I came across a picture of you online, just two days ago. It's been the most agonizingly long wait of my life to see you in person. And, in person, it's ten times worse. You are beautiful. I'm one hundred percent interested in you. I want to take you out on a date or on a walk or whatever you want to do. And, I'm sorry to tell you this, but I don't care what your sister thinks. I hope that's not offensive. But, I have to put it out there. I want to get to know you, Mary."

There. He'd said it. All that he wanted to say. And even if this weekend was just one big tease, or if this weekend resulted in a couple subsequent phone calls or texts that went nowhere, he had to try. Even his own failed marriage had never felt as electric as the little interactions he was having with Mary. Kurt didn't know if he believed in love at first sight, but he started to think that he didn't *not* believe in it.

Mary took it all in. She looked a little hurt, for some reason, but she didn't get up. She didn't run this time. Instead, she blinked and then took his hand back in hers.

"I like you, too, Kurt." She said. "But, I love my sister. I'm sorry. I have to see if she is okay."

# Chapter 33

Mary was smitten. Kurt was handsome and smart and said all the right things.

Almost.

She understood that he could easily set aside Anna's feelings. And she also understood that Anna was being unreasonable.

Hearing about the vision Kurt had for the weekend conflicted with what Anna had pitched. Sure, Anna emphasized that FantasyCoin wanted to get away from it all. Relax. Commune with nature. All those romantic expectations city folk had of spending less than 48 hours in Maplewood.

But Anna had also said that Kurt was going to play it cool, be professional. She even heard Anna say it *to* Kurt. She was trying to control a situation in which there was no point in having control. Kurt didn't seem to care if things got a little wild. Her sister had missed the mark. But she was still Mary's sister. She had to make sure things were okay between them.

Mary stood from the sofa, smoothed her shirt and smiled down at Kurt.

"Yeah, you should go see if she is okay," he said as he stood next to her. He seemed like he didn't know what to do with his hands and awkwardly tucked them into his back pockets. He nodded to her and smiled back.

She could feel Kurt's eyes on her as she stepped to the love seat and pulled the flannel blanket from its back. Once she had folded it over her arm, she moved back in his direction to get to the door.

Mary squeezed between Kurt and the coffee table as she muttered, "Excuse me." Her back brushed him and their electricity jolted her. Before she opened the door to go out, she turned to him and said, "Maybe we can talk more in the morning? I would hate for you to wait for me. This could take a while."

Kurt's face fell a little, and Mary's heart clenched. Suddenly and without warning, she crossed back to him and stopped. He furrowed his brow, his hands still propped in his back pockets.

Mary placed her right hand on his chest, pushed up onto her toes, and brushed her lips against his cheek, just above his beard. Once she began to drop back down, he grabbed her left hand and gave it a squeeze.

She started to move again to the door but he pulled her back and drew her hand to his mouth, kissing the smooth back of her petite hand.

Mary felt dizzy. Kurt steadied her and then said, "Go on. Sisters come first." Mary smiled, her eyes crinkling at the corners.

Reluctantly, she edged away, feeling on top of the world. Mary could feel Kurt's eyes on her, as she left him at the sofa.

It was now time to smooth things over with Anna. She opened the door and stepped into the frigid night. Her breath collected in the air ahead of her as she wrapped her arms around herself and headed down the steps toward the fire.

Anna was sitting on the bench stump that Mary had scrabbled together for the weekend. The others had moved their stumps a bit closer to the fire pit, huddling for warmth. Jace and Eddie were still working on cigars. Rory was making the last of the 'smores that Mary had set out. Maci was still, somehow, fixed on the glow from her phone, her pink fingers flashing out from her sweatshirt sleeves. Kato and Alex stood to head inside. It wasn't very late, yet. But, it was bitterly cold out. The flatlanders had just about gotten their fill already, Mary thought. She moved to the side to let the two pass.

"Thanks for a delicious dinner, Mary," Kato nodded at her.

"And the terrific accommodations. I can't remember the last time I sat around a campfire. And I don't think I have ever sat around a campfire in *snow*," Alex gushed.

"I hope you didn't get any frostbite!" Mary cheerfully replied. "Feel free to warm up inside for a while before bed. There are a few decks of cards and board games in the front hall closet. Help yourselves if you aren't ready to hit the sack." The two nodded and thanked her and hobbled their way back up the slippery steps, holding onto the railings for support.

"Hi, Mary!" Maci looked up and slid her phone into the front pocket of her sweatshirt. "How's your hot water? Should we be mindful of staggering our showers?"

"Oh, no. Have at it. The lodge is well-equipped with enough tanks to provide about a dozen simultaneous hot showers. Go wild," Mary assured her.

"Cool! I'll see you in the morning! I'm getting a little sleepy," Maci yawned as if to prove she had better scuttle her way to her room.

"Breakfast at about nine, and then we'll have our first activity," Mary called after Maci as she slipped her way up the steps.

The others carried on in their conversation, letting Mary finally settle down onto the knobby log next to Anna. Anna didn't look at Mary. She kept her eyes trained on the fire, mesmerized by the slowly dying flames.

"Here," Mary offered, "Let me revive this a bit." And she pulled a small log from behind where they were sitting and fed it to the hungry fire. She picked up the long stick that Kato had been using as a stoker and prodded the embers, giving the fire new life.

"Wanna talk?" She said in a low voice to her sister's profile.

"Not really," Anna responded, glancing at Rory, Jace, and Eddie, who were starting to stub out their cigars.

"We're going to join Kato and Alex inside. My fingers are numb," Eddie said to the girls. Mary gave them a wave and a smile before wrapping her hand back under her red and black checkered blanket. Once everyone had gone in, she stood and fanned the blanket out and around Anna and herself, cuddling her sister into her.

"Thanks," Anna sniffed. Mary knew Anna. If she waited quietly long enough, it would all spill out. Several moments passed. The fresh log Mary added to the fire began to crisp as the flames ate away.

Finally, Anna shifted. "It's just," Mary was right, here it came. "It's just that I guess I have always had a little crush on Kurt. But it's never something I would have acted on. I knew that doing that would not only compromise my career but also jeopardize FantasyCoin. It's a very fragile business in an equally-fragile industry. I care a lot about work. I know that not everyone does."

Mary waited as Anna squashed fresh snow under her boot. "I mean, do you? I thought you were more invested in the Lodge than this," Anna looked up at her sister and passed her hand out around her.

"Ann, I can be invested in the Lodge and still have blood flowing through my veins."

"So you really like Kurt all of a sudden? How did this even happen? What do you think you're going to get out of this, anyway? Kurt lives in the valley. He owns a condo. He's divorced. He literally works on a computer all day. You don't even own one. Do you really think this is going to go well for you, Mary?" Anna leaned away from her sister and gave her a sidelong look. It was critical and judgmental and scornful, and Mary regretted even coming out.

"Forget this," Mary stood and brushed off the seat of her pants. She let the blanket fall off her back and onto the empty log. "You say that women should chase their dreams, but you have forgotten that other women have different dreams than you. Good night, Anna."

And with that, Mary marched inside, through the living room, bidding the others goodnight before she marched up the staircase and into her own room. She pulled her clothes off and left them to wilt in a pile by the bed as she shrugged her nightgown onto her body. She crawled into bed and clicked off her lamp. And once dark fell over the pinewood-covered room, she noticed a little glow from her phone on the nightstand.

1 unread message.

# Chapter 34

Kurt had gone up to his room to check his phone for service there. Once he made his way to the outlet behind the nightstand, he plugged it in and woke it up. One measly bar.

*Better than nothing,* he thought. He went to the bathroom and splashed some cool water over his face. He thought of brushing his teeth and calling it a night until he heard a roar of laughter hum through the floor. He figured he had better go join the others. After all, this *was* a FantasyCoin retreat, despite the fact that, for him, it was turning into something much, much bigger.

But before he went down to the great room, he grabbed for his phone. When he neared his door, he saw that he lost the signal, so he traced his steps back to the bedside. Once the bar popped back up, he pulled up his messages and began to compose a new one.

Sweet dreams, beautiful Mary.

He kept it simple and plugged the phone back in before deciding to head downstairs. He liked the thrill of hoping he'd get a response before bedtime, and keeping the phone tied up in his room would force him to wait.

He trotted down the stairs as his group of employees laughed again in tandem. He saw that they were scattered around the coffee table playing a card game with what looked like spoons. Anna wasn't there. Mary wasn't there. Maci wasn't there. All guys.

"Hey-o, Boss-man!" Eddie clapped and cheered as Kurt made his way into their game.

"Hey, hey. What are you nerds playing?" Kurt loved to rib the other guys, even though he knew full well he was the ultimate nerd.

"Spoons," Jace chimed in. "When we were little, we would go to the White Mountains to ski in the winter. My mom would always force us into playing this cutthroat game. My sisters and I loved it, even though it usually ended in tears or even blood," Jace explained as he doled out another round.

"*Blood?*" Alex asked. "That's legit. My parents hardly even let us bleed. My dad was so scared we would get hurt playing outside and sometimes even inside that I don't think I had my first actual injury until my late teenage years."

The guys laughed again. Kurt had never heard them let loose like this, despite the fact that they were still relatively tame.

"Okay, okay, so time out," Rory interjected. "You guys gotta tell Kurt about Kato's *list!*" Another round of cheers went up. They were so loud that Kurt was worried that they would wake the girls upstairs, assuming the girls were asleep. But he couldn't shush them. He was too interested in the bro talk to be a mother hen. He needed this retreat as much as his employees did. Maybe more.

"Oh, no. Here we go! Lay it on me," Kurt laughed at Rory and sank back into the overstuffed love seat next to Alex. As Rory regaled Kurt in a tale of Kato's lovesickness over the receptionist in their building, Kurt felt himself grow more and more tired.

The game of spoons was suspended while the others settled back into the sofas or stretched out onto the rug. The fire was almost out entirely, and the drafty pinewood room was cooling down, uncomfortably. When Rory had finished his tales of unrequited love and Kato had confirmed it all, nodding his head sadly but smiling, Jace jumped up.

"It's freezing in here, man," he started darting around the room, feeling along the walls and peeking into the nooks and crannies, apparently for a thermostat. "Do you think Mary keeps it below 60 or something? Should one of us tend the fire through the night?" His worry was genuine, causing a few of the others to laugh at him.

"Nah, don't bother with that. I'm sure the rooms are warmer. This is probably our cue to hit the hay, gentlemen," Kurt commanded. He felt exhausted and wanted to encourage the others to quiet down and settle in.

They all agreed. Rory boxed the cards. Alex collected the spoons and stored them in a mason jar in the middle of the coffee table like a little centerpiece. They each said their goodnights as they summited the staircase and went their separate ways down the long hall.

As Kurt slid his key into the keyhole on his door, he saw Anna pass behind him out of the corner of his eye. He swiveled around.

"Anna! I had no idea you were still out there. You must be freezing. Are you okay?" She didn't do him the courtesy of stopping. Instead, she passed right on by and tucked her own key into Mary's door as she choked out a quick reply.

"Being raised on the mountain gives you a different tolerance for some things, Kurt. I can stand a little chill. Some people can't, I guess." She looked over her shoulder at him and smirked just as she turned the key and swung the door open.

He ignored her confusing comment and instead caught a flash inside the room. He thought he saw Mary's slight shape under the covers of a modest little iron-framed bed. She was faced away and her phone was glowing out from her hands. She didn't turn when Anna opened the door, and Kurt didn't want to be caught peaking. So he pressed himself into his own room and quickly and quietly shut his door behind him, resting against it for a moment.

And just then, a little light blinked awake on his cell phone.

# Chapter 35

Breakfast is at nine. Hot cakes. To eat, that is.

Mary suppressed a giggle as she pressed send and curled the phone to her chest under the heavy wool blanket.

"Hi."

Mary shot up and almost fell out of bed. It was Anna, scaring her to death with her quiet entrance. "Didn't mean to scare you. Thought you heard me when I unlocked the door."

"No," was all Mary replied. She still felt cool toward her sister. The fireside remarks were unnecessary and bordered on cruel. She still had nothing to say to Anna.

She turned off her phone and slipped it under her pillow before snuggling back down in her little spot on the left side of the bed. Mary then closed her eyes and chose to ignore her sister.

It wasn't easy. She was forced to listen as Anna unzipped her jeans more loudly than seemed natural, stomped into the bathroom, and turned the shower on.

Mary was then forced to breathe in the steam that curled out from under the bathroom door as Anna took the world's longest shower.

Then, Mary had to listen on as Anna brushed her teeth with an electric toothbrush for what seemed like ten minutes. At this point, Mary joined her phone under the pillow.

Finally, Anna emerged from the bathroom, taking her time in shutting off the light, but then continuing the disruption by waving around her cell phone's flashlight to guide herself to bed, despite the short distance.

Mary's irritation swelled to the point that she considered marching downstairs and sleeping on the sofa. And she would if she wouldn't risk being caught by one of the guests. It would be decidedly unprofessional to be found sleeping on a couch in the great room- even more unprofessional than flirting with one of the guests, she reasoned.

Finally, Anna flipped back the covers, exposing Mary's upper body to the 60 degrees at which she had set the thermostat. It seemed to take another ten minutes for Anna to finally pull the covers over her own body, but leaving Mary still partially exposed. Mary shrugged herself back into the covers and snuggled back down.

Her sister's rear-end bumped into her own. She couldn't help but giggle. Anna didn't giggle back, though.

Mary felt like they were little girls again, sharing their bed in the farmhouse all those years ago. It felt barely bigger than a twin bed, however. She and Anna had shared it as long as Mary could remember. All the way until Anna left for college the summer after she graduated high school.

When Anna had left, it took Mary a very long time to get used to sleeping alone. She would sometimes even find herself crawling into Alan's bed in the room next door. He was a good six years younger than her, but he had his own bed since he was the only boy left at home.

Mary could even remember a particular night when Alan must have slept over at a neighbor's house. She crawled into bed with her mother in the middle of the night. She was a full sixteen years old, and there she was, trying to sleep in bed with her parents. Her mother shooed her out before daylight, making it the longest night of Mary's night.

She couldn't explain her sleepless nights except to say that she got lonely and scared. It took months before she finally worked herself into the habit of sleeping by herself. That was how she got into reading. She had to find a way to tire herself out well enough that she wasn't lonely or frightened. Books offered her company and comfort. They carried her through the rest of high school and into the two years she spent trudging back and forth between the junior college that she commuted to in nearby Lowell.

By the time Mary had earned her Associate's Degree in Business, she had probably read two dozen books on hospitality and real estate investment. At that point, Anna had already graduated from college and agreed to co-sign with Mary on the loan for the Lodge. It wasn't too hard to get, because the lodge was offered well below what it was probably worth.

As she lay there in bed, her back accidentally colliding with Anna's as they both tried to get comfortable, she felt sad for how the day had ended and how her patience for her sister had run out. She reached her hand back and searched for her sister's arm. When she found it, she tickled it and whispered, "I love you, Annie."

Minutes later, as Mary was finally drifting off to sleep, she heard a quiet mumble from behind her.

"Love you, Mare."

# Chapter 36

In the busyness of the previous night, Mary had forgotten to pull down the wooden blinds and draw the beige flannel curtains. The morning light poured into her room and onto her sleeping face, waking her up ahead of her alarm. She threw her arm over her eyes, willing herself back to sleep before she remembered everything that had happened. She did a mental catalog. Heavy flirting with Kurt. Check. Fight with Anna. Check. On the road to making up with Anna. Check. The entire rest of the retreat and the other (equally important) guests. Eh. Mary needed to refocus, at least for breakfast.

She rolled out of bed and peeked over at Anna, who was out to the world. She was snoring loudly, her mouth agape, limbs splayed in every direction. It amazed Mary that her sister's notorious bed thrashing hadn't woken her before the sunlight had. She quickly pulled the blinds and drew the drapes on each side of the bed, hoping that Anna would get to sleep a while longer.

Then, she made her way into the shower, where she lathered with her yummy-smelling homemade rosemary-lavender soap. She washed her hair and applied a cream rinse before finishing up and getting out. She smoothed on some body lotion before shrugging on her robe and towel drying her hair.

Mary cracked the bathroom door and looked out to see if Anna had woken up. Still snoring. She gently closed the door and got to work on brushing her teeth and applying a little makeup. Not ten minutes later, she checked again on Anna. Still asleep. Mary wanted to blow dry her hair, but she dared not awaken the sleeping dragon.

So, she decided she'd have to go with the damp look, and she went to her closet to pull out a fresh outfit. She wore something similar to the day before, but this time she selected a snugger pair of jeans. Pulling them past her butt was somewhat of a struggle, but she was reassured when she zipped them without a hitch. She then buttoned on a comfy, casual flannel top and slid into her worn leather house slippers. She figured she'd save the boots for when it was time to go into the woods.

She gave herself a once over in her full-length mirror and, despite her damp hair, felt good enough to start on breakfast. If Anna woke up and came down before Kurt, she would scramble back up to dry her hair and fix it. If not, then he'd just get to see her au natural. She didn't mind, though. Her hair was full enough and her hairline flattering enough that it sort of looked cute when it was wet and undone.

Before heading downstairs, she checked her phone to see that there were no more messages from Kurt. A little deflated, she moved around the bed and pulled the blankets back up over her sister, who snorted in the middle of a snore. It felt a little like a "thank you," and Mary giggled to herself. Today she and Anna would make things better. She had a good feeling.

She left the room, closing the door silently as she went. When she passed Kurt's door, she hesitated, trying to see if she could hear anything on the other side. When no sounds came, she made her way to the staircase and down to the kitchen.

Once the coffee was percolating, Mary counted out nine mugs and set one aside for herself. She took the other eight out to the table and set them in the top right corner of each place mat, double checking for leftover crumbs from last night.

She then went back to the kitchen and pulled her extra-large cast iron pan onto the front of the stove before igniting the coordinating burner. She added in a chunk of cold butter from the fridge and set the burner to low as she pulled together ingredients for Mama's Mountain Flapjacks.

Once she poured the first cup of batter into the pan, she served herself some coffee, added her sugar, and dashed out to the reception to turn on her Christmas music. She ran back into the kitchen to see she made it just in time to flip the first pancake.

She sipped her coffee and continued to steadily flip through a mounting pile of pancakes when she remembered the bacon. Checking the time, she saw it was nearing 8:45. She preheated the oven, scattered some bacon across two wide baking sheets and shoved them in.

By nine o'clock, the group began to trickle down the stairs, sleepily, despite the late hour.

She held her breath as she heard the first two traipse down toward the great room. She cocked her head out of the kitchen to see, hoping it might be Kurt. She had silently wished he'd come a little early, giving them time to chat. But, it wasn't. Instead, it was Alex and Jace, who had decided to remain in their pajamas.

"Morning, guys! Help yourself to some coffee. Breakfast is almost ready," Mary called to them, cheerily. Soon after, Maci and Eddie joined, looking a little worse for wear in their nightclothes, too.

"Hello, you two! Come grab some coffee. Did you sleep well?" Mary felt happy to have such a full house. It felt a little like when she was a girl and her mom would make a big hearty breakfast on Christmas Eve.

"Morning, Mary," Maci yawned and cut through the kitchen and into the dining room.

"Man, I don't remember the last time I slept so well," Eddie commented. Mary smiled. Almost every guest in the history of Wood Smoke Lodge had said the same thing. Mary thought it was because the flatlanders didn't realize the value of sleeping in a cooler climate. But the beds and bedding were really quite cozy, too.

Finally she saw Kurt and Anna descend the stairs together with Rory and Kate just behind them. Kurt's eyes looked heavy, and Anna seemed quiet.

"Morning!" Rory called from behind them. "Coffee, by chance?" He asked as he scooted ahead of the others.

"Absolutely, it must be urgent. Mugs are on the table. Help yourself," Mary directed, keeping her eye on Kurt and Anna. Anna cut away and headed to the reception area, where the music was playing. Kurt ambled on and into the kitchen, pulling up right next to her.

"Morning," he said in a low voice.

# Chapter 37

Kurt saw Mary's face flicker up as "Jingle Bells" came on the CD player from the reception. She dropped her head again and smiled, wryly. Anna had changed the song. It was a subtle message to Mary that she was still upset.

"How's Anna this morning?" Mary asked him.

"Didn't you two share a room last night?" He felt his eyebrow creep up in reply.

"Yeah, well. If it isn't obvious by her music sabotage act just now," she laughed, then caught herself and glanced up from her pancake-flipping to see if Anna had come in. She didn't finish her sentence.

"Who doesn't like 'Jingle Bells?'" He returned, incredulous. He may not be a Christmas guru, but Kurt loved holiday music. In fact, the Christmas theme was a driving force in his decision to choose Mary's lodge for the retreat. At least, it was a driving force until he had caught a glimpse of her picture. That's what sealed the deal.

Mary laughed again, this time more heartily. "Hey, this is *my* CD. I love *all* Christmas music. But I also know when my own sister is trying to get under my skin."

"Is it working?" Kurt started. "Because you do seem to be a little worked up."

"It's not Anna or the music that is having that effect." Mary flopped the last pancake onto a towering stack next to the stove, set the spatula down, crossed her arms, and looked up at him. She batted her full lashes at him once or twice and her lips curled up. Kurt could hardly stand it.

"If only you knew the effect *you* have on *me*," he mumbled and started to reach for a strand of her hair that had fallen forward onto her cheek.

"Wow."

By then, they should have counted on Anna to interrupt.

"Anyway," she continued as Mary and Kurt each swiveled away from each other. Kurt stepped toward the dining room and Mary hefted up the precarious plate of hotcakes for delivery. "How'd you sleep, Mare?" Anna splashed coffee into her mug and began to sip at it as she followed her sister to the dining room.

"Fine. And you?" Mary replied over her shoulder.

Kurt took his place at the far end of the right-hand bench again and watched as the sisters nimbly navigated around the room. Mary leaned over the head of the table and positioned the plate squarely onto a hot pad on the table's end.

"Bacon's coming right up, but go ahead and dig into the cakes," she placed a hand on each hip as she surveyed her handiwork. "Oh, Jace, syrup's right here," she pointed to a squat white pitcher. "Butter in the glass butter dish on the far side down there by Kurt," she looked right at him, bold as could be. She held his gaze and ran her tongue up over her upper lip, but only barely.

He sucked in a breath.

"What is it?" Eddie shot a look at him as if he was choking.

"Oh, nothing. Everything looks delicious, Mary. Thank you so much. I should have asked, do you need any help with bacon?" Mary started to reply and then Anna appeared, perching over her left shoulder.

"Um, no, but thank you," she smiled. "You all eat up. We have a busy morning ahead of us. You'll need your strength. I promise you that." Mary winked at them and spun around to go tend to the bacon.

The rest of the group dug in, thoroughly enjoying their second hearty, down-home meal.

"So, any word from the temps in the valley, Kurt? How's business going? I don't think I have had so much time away from my phone or computer. I feel completely out-of-touch. Do any of you even have cell service?" Eddie asked through mouthfuls.

"I barely have service. I had to resort to cleaning up my photos and playing solitaire offline. It's the hardest vacation I have ever been on," she whined, but Kurt could see a smile prick at the corner of her mouth.

"You're ridiculous," Eddie laughed.

"I have a little bit of cell service in my room, actually," Kurt said. "And I hate to admit this, but," he pressed on, as the group looked at him like they do during company meetings. "I tried to check my email once, earlier yesterday, and have forgotten about it since."

He took his napkin and wiped at his mouth. The group stared back him, almost nervously. Then, Eddie started a slow clap. It caught on, and the rest of the table chimed in, cheering that Kurt had basically forgotten about the most important thing in his life.

Or was it? He smiled broadly back at his staff but saw that Anna was not clapping or smiling. In fact, she was about to interrupt their applause. But, just as she opened her mouth, Mary broke into the dining room, humming along to "Silver Bells" as it echoed throughout the lodge. In her toweled hands was a steaming baking sheet.

"Bacon!" She sang out.

The group turned their cheer onto Mary and her tray of glistening slices of greasy delight. Kurt was distracted, however, by Anna and whatever she wanted to say about work. He waited and watched Mary as she clipped little bunches of slices with her tongs and dropped them onto plates, one by one.

He couldn't help but to notice her outfit. The easy way she wore the flannel button-down. Her skin-tight jeans with the slightest hint of a rip on the front of her upper thigh. He's eyes skimmed back up to her top as she came down his side of the bench. Was it just him or was her shirt unbuttoned a little farther down than he had remembered? He saw her catch him looking, and his face flushed.

"Eat your heart out," she winked down at him as she clicked her tongs open onto his plate.

"Thanks," he panted.

Mary turned to go. The cheers had finally subsided, and the group was gobbling up the crispy spindles.

"I'll bring back the pot of coffee for seconds and then let you all digest your breakfast. Afterwards, we'll meet in the great room at about 10:30," she smiled at everyone and pivoted toward the kitchen.

When she left, Kurt turned his head to Anna. She had her arms crossed, pointedly ignoring the bacon Mary had heaped on her plate. He needed to bring her back into the fold.

"Anna, were you going to say something earlier?" He offered her the opportunity to vent or chime in or do whatever she needed to do to rejoin them. She snapped her head toward him. Slowly, her mouth twisted into a smile.

116

"Well, yes, actually. About FantasyCoin," she started, looking around the table to see if the others would give her their attention, too.

"Go ahead, please. At least one of us is sensible enough to maintain some degree of reality," he joked. But his unease grew when Anna pursed her lips.

"Reality; good way to put it." Anna considered herself for a moment. Maci laughed nervously. When Kurt looked at Maci, he saw that she was eyeing Anna like a cat.

Anna continued, carefully. "I was able to get into my email last night when I was out at the fire. Dave, our off-site analyst, indicated that everything was smooth sailing with operations," she paused, looking again to see that everyone was watching her. "But," she stopped. Kurt felt his stomach flip. Maybe he'd been careless with this retreat idea. What did Anna find out?

"Go on," he prompted.

"But the market has taken an early downturn. It's not good news, that's for sure. Dave had originally predicted we'd be on safe ground until a week before Christmas. It seems like we were lucky to make it so far past Black Friday. Our value has dropped by 15% since yesterday. That's obviously dramatic. Dave is guessing that we are going to start following the pattern of Bitcoin and Ethereum after all. Of course, we have every reason to hope that things will ratchet back up after the new year and especially once tax season gets rolling."

"Wait a minute," Kurt held his hand up. "Anna, this sounds like a well-prepared report. Did you two chat at length? Is there some sort of crisis we need to brace for? Contextualize this for us a bit. I mean, is there an actual reason here to ruin our trip? It's just begun, after all," he waved his hand around the room, trying to remind Anna of how much everyone seemed to be enjoying themselves.

"It's not good, Kurt," Anna responded flatly.

# Chapter 38

Mary had returned with the coffee, but the mood of the room had shifted dramatically in the few moments she had been gone. Anna was lecturing the others. Kurt's face had an edge to it. Eddie wasn't even smiling. Maci's face was drawn, too. Though she knew very little about the digital world and far less about digital currency, she had enough sense to understand basic finance.

"I don't mean to ruin the trip, of course," Anna looked over at Mary. She seemed a little sad, Mary thought. "I did end up calling and chatting with him late last night when I read his email. Of course there is little we can or would do even if we were at the office. Marketing has very limited effect on the impending downturn. We already knew this was coming, after all. We just thought we would have another solid week of strong numbers and maybe even some growth."

Mary had no idea what the numbers would be, but of course she understood that FantasyCoin had been outperforming its competitors recently. Anna had tried to explain to her that it was because FantasyCoin provided a relatively tangible service- fantasy football teams ran their leagues through it. Anna was under the impression that FantasyCoin would remain stable in the market during football season, which was far from over. She was genuinely curious about why it would suffer a crash.

"Anna," she moved behind the bench and leaned on the side table behind it. "I thought that FantasyCoin would hang in there all the way until the Super Bowl. How could the holidays affect it?"

"It's not about the product or service. That's solid. The numbers Dave is referencing have to do with people who invest in the currency, not the service. They are two separate things. Yes, you'd think they'd be connected, but for the last few years, there has been a classic pattern during November and December. Investors cash out to pay for Christmas. It's pretty simple." Anna didn't even turn around to look at her, and her voice pitched up in irritation.

"Well, is this going to affect your stay here? What could you possibly do to improve the outcome?"

Jace, Rory, and Alex turned to Mary, their faces pleading as if to encourage her to continue to shut Anna down. Mary never thought of Anna as a Debbie Downer, but she was starting to act like one.

"We can't do anything, but I'll be frank, Mary. It's frustrating that you have no internet, no cell service, not even television. We all feel disconnected and powerless. It's uncomfortable, right?" Anna looked to the others to garner support.

"No," Kurt replied immediately. "We are enjoying this trip. Anna, I can understand if you feel that way, I suppose. But, then again, you are the one who insisted we try this out. Get away from it all. Unplug. Unwind? Remember? It would be good for the company to commune a little?"

"I know what I said, Kurt," Anna cut him off. "But that was in the context of our riding high so late into the season."

Mary needed to intercede. "Anna, Kurt- you're the bosses. Maybe you two ought to have a little conference on this. In the meantime, I'd love to get everyone else set up for our first team-building exercise." Mary pinned her fists to her sides.

When Anna didn't turn around and Kurt just looked at her helplessly, she continued. "Okay, Alex, Jace, Rory, Maci, Eddie, Kato- head to your rooms and get bundled up. If you have gloves or boots, you'll need them. I'll clear the dishes. Meet me back down in the great room in about fifteen."

The group didn't argue. And except for Maci tapping away at her cell phone and Eddie whispering something to Kato, they left quietly, trudging up the stairs like sullen children.

Mary began to clear the table, dropping utensils into the coffee mugs and stacking the plates. She planned to carry about her business.

If Kurt and Anna wanted privacy to talk business, they could step out. Mary had a retreat to run. She delivered the first haul into the kitchen and returned.

"Mary, I'd like your opinion here," Kurt stood and shuffled out from behind his bench. He leaned against the wall.

"My opinion? I won't be any help," Mary nervously replied.

"Now that I can agree with," Anna chirped. "What would Mary have to say? It's not as if I'm asking for an opinion here. I'm just expressing concern with the fact that we are completely isolated. It wasn't something I had thought would be an issue, but I was wrong."

"Mary's a businesswoman. She knows the basics of tending to business emergencies. Mary," Kurt went on, "If you were away from the Lodge, and Anna was running it for you, and... let's say a pipe burst and the guests had to evacuate and stay elsewhere. You maybe would even need to cover their expenses on that. Well, then, here are my questions. 1. Would you want Anna to be able to get in touch with you for advice? 2. Would you return home to support her in handling it?" He crossed his arms and cocked his head at Mary.

Mary couldn't tell what his angle was, but he sounded sincere. The answers were obvious, though. "I'd feel bad she couldn't get in touch with me, and I would return to help. But it's not comparable, Kurt. And anyway, Anna, what do you think needs to happen? What is your real concern here? Does this analyst guy need your help? Does he need to be able to reach you- any of you?" Mary looked earnestly at her sister, who was still slumped on the bench.

Anna played with the bacon on her plate.

"There is nothing any one of us could do to help Dave or the company for that matter. The market will do what it will do. I just," she trailed off, staring out the bay window. Snow flurries had begun to fall.

"Kurt? I think it's clear that Anna isn't saying any of you need to go home. But, maybe let us sisters talk for a while?" Kurt nodded his head and pushed off from the wall. He looked down at Anna and then smiled at Mary.

"Absolutely. Anna, before I go I want you to know how much I respect you professionally. It's vital we have someone like you to present us with the facts. I support whatever direction you think we should take- if you think we need to give Dave some directives on amping up marketing, if you think we should make a trip into town and spend some time on the phone, whatever. But, I don't think any of us need to forego this weekend." He clapped his hands together. "Okay, I'll see ya in a bit."

Mary watched as he strode away past the fireplace, into the great room and then up the stairs.

Mary took a seat next to Anna. "I know this is about Kurt and me, and I'm sorry for that. I'm sorry it's causing you so much stress."

"It's more than that, Mare," Anna's voice softened considerably. "I really do want FantasyCoin to sustain itself through this month. I didn't remember just how isolated you are out here. It's giving me anxiety to be out of the loop. And, besides, I do just feel…" she shifted her weight and opened toward Mary, "uncomfortable."

"Were you in love with Kurt? Tell me truthfully, Anna. Because if you were, I'll back off right now. No bones about it." Mary meant every word. She had never had the sense that Anna was interested in her boss, until Mary herself became interested.

"No. Ew. No, not love. Just… I like Kurt as a person, I guess. He's decent. He isn't the type of guy who I am used to meeting. And besides that, I don't know, Mare. I have never seen you like this. So *into* somebody. It's weird. And Kurt isn't your type. If he's anyone's type, he's mine. I mean we freaking have the same job, basically. Live in the same city." Anna trailed off and looked back outside again. Mary covered her sister's hand.

"Anna, I refuse to step on your toes. But, I'm not convinced I'm stepping on them. Do you just want to claim Kurt because you saw that I was attracted to him?"

"Mary, I have no idea. This whole thing just isn't what I envisioned. I envisioned bringing you business and keeping our own expense account in order. Meeting Kurt's expectations. Doing what was best for everyone."

Mary considered this for a moment. Finally, she asked her sister, "Did you ever stop to think about what was best for you?"

# Chapter 39

Kurt had pulled his black beanie over his head and strapped into the winter boots he'd found in the depths of his closet. He then grabbed the ski jacket he'd packed at the last minute.

He thought about Mary and Anna. How he was impressed that Mary seemed to be able to deescalate Anna so smoothly. He had noticed that Mary was firm but gentle, and he thought about how he'd seen other women in his life handle situations like that.

Brittany was hot-tempered and impatient. She would blow up and rush off. Early in their relationship, he thought her fiery reactions were sexy. Of course, they ended up getting old fast.

And as for the other woman in his life, his mom, well, he rarely saw her deal with conflict. In fact, he rarely saw his mom at all. Despite the fact that she had raised him, they were not a close family. She was often at the tennis courts or the spa or shopping. The few times he saw his mother become upset, she would end up ignoring the matter entirely.

Mary was decidedly different.

Kurt adjusted the beanie down lower over his forehead and strode over to the nightstand where he'd left his phone. He had muted notifications for the weekend, other than texts. He had no texts, but he figured he had time to check his email and read the market analysis Anna had referenced.

Ninety-seven unread emails populated. Instead of starting at the top with most recent, he scrolled down and searched for yesterday's date. He spotted Dave's email right away.

Anna had exaggerated somewhat. Their numbers were down fourteen percent, rather than fifteen. But when he opened Dave's second attachment he saw a cross-reference for competing coins. Almost every other one was down well over twenty percent. He breathed out a small sigh of relief and began to close his email app before he decided to peruse the more recent ones for any updates.

Scrolling slowly through admin emails and a few spam messages, he saw Dave's name again toward the top of the page.

Dave Durbin          URGENT- ACTION REQUIRED          9:31 AM

"Oh jeez," Kurt muttered, clicking open the email.

*Hey guys- tried to call. No luck. Bad news. Back-up server failed. Need oversight ASAP. Hate to ruin the trip, but could use one of you down here stat, just in case. - Dave*

As Kurt was reading the brief email, a text message cut across the screen. It was also from Dave. It was an almost identical message. Kurt was crestfallen. He could not abort the retreat. They had barely gotten there. And, he couldn't abort the mission with Mary.

Then he had an idea. He popped his phone off the charger and scrambled downstairs. As he skipped down the last few steps, he saw Anna and Mary clearing away the last few dishes from breakfast.

"Anna, did you see this yet?" He was stalking toward her, his phone stretched out in front of him as if she could read the tiny screen from yards away.

"No?" She stopped, holding her own syrupy plate between her hands. Her face scrunched, and she tried to make out the small font as he neared. When he was within arm's reach, she squinted at his phone and read the text he had open.

"You've got to be kidding me. Bad timing with the market turn," she looked up at him, her jaw set. "Kurt, we have to go back. We can't afford to lose servers. Has Dave called in support staff? Did you talk to him?" She pressed.

"No, I only just read it. One of us needs to be there to give the green light on who to bring in and oversee the work." He stopped and glanced over at Mary, who was holding two coffee mugs. Her expression unreadable.

He looked at Anna, his eyes pleading. "Will you go for us?"

Anna flicked a glance to her sister and back to Kurt. She released the plate with one hand and propped her free hand on her hip. After a beat, she replied.

"Of course. Without a doubt."

"That's why I hired you, Anna," Kurt smiled broadly, shifting his gaze to Mary briefly. "I'll help you pack up. You can take my car. Maci and I can catch a ride home with the others," he instructed. He felt himself shift to business mode.

"What's going on?"

Kurt whipped around to see Maci reaching the landing of the steps and crossing over to them. "Back-up servers failed? Do we all need to leave? I mean, some of the guys would be able to handle this in no time," she suggested, glancing from Kurt to Anna and back.

"No, no. Anna just needs to be there to make some financial calls on hiring out and making sure it gets done. She is more than capable," Kurt nodded at Anna, who seemed to beam back at him, proudly.

"I'd be happy to join you, Anna. If you want some company?"

"No need, Maci. I'm sure you want to be part of the team-building stuff, right?" Anna offered a soft look back at Mary. Kurt noticed that worry was starting to creep into Mary's face.

"Well it's up to the two of you. Either way, I'm sure the team-building activities will work out fine," he offered a small smile to Mary.

"I'll stay, then. But only if Anna is cool with driving down alone, especially in the snow."

"I've made the drive for years," Anna reassured all of them. Kurt felt good. He thought this might be exactly what everyone needed, especially Anna. But he wanted to make sure he wasn't isolating her, and he wasn't sure how to address it.

"Anna, let's talk for a moment before you get ready to go," he said in a low voice and began to walk toward the reception area and out of the way. The others were starting to march downstairs in their mismatched snow gear.

Once Anna had joined him by the front desk, he started in. "Anna, I really appreciate you doing this. I just want to make sure you won't feel left out or that I *don't want* you to be here," his eyebrows knitted together in worry as he propped his elbow up on the desk and leaned onto his hand.

"Kurt, honestly. This is actually perfect. I think I need to get out of here. With you and Mary hitting it off, it's... well... uncomfortable for me. I have never seen you in that light. I have never even seen Mary in that light. And, what's more is that I really am stressed about being so disconnected. I was just telling this to Mary, actually," she waved her hand absently in the direction of the kitchen.

"FantasyCoin will be fine. And I'm sorry to make you feel awkward, but I don't mean to," he replied evenly.

"Yeah, I know. Still, this is the right thing. For everyone. I think Mary needs the space. I think *I* need the space. And, this will make me feel good about ensuring that the retreat doesn't derail our success."

Kurt started to cut in, but Anna held up her hand. "I know. I know you think this retreat is going to *support* our success. But, I have always thought it was a little irresponsible to go totally dark. So this is good. This is very good." Suddenly Anna moved toward Kurt and hugged him.

It caught him off guard. He wrapped one arm around her and then leaned back, his eyes searching hers suspiciously.

"What was that?"

"Just a little goodbye. I'll see you back at the office. Monday morning. Bright and early. Back to normal, right?" She smiled and headed up the stairs, not waiting for him to reply.

# Chapter 40

Mary quickly set the mugs in the sink, wiped her hands on an errant dish towel and all but ran after Anna and up the stairs, ignoring Kurt.

Once she reached the top landing, she looked down at him, bit her lip and gave him a broad smile. She felt like he knew what he was doing. It seemed like a win-win: fix the FantasyCoin server thing and let Anna off the hook emotionally. Mary had never seen a man assess a situation so coolly and effectively.

He grinned back up at her, but there was a kind of hesitation in his eyes. If he was questioning himself, Mary liked him even better. She plodded down the hall and broke into her room.

Anna was bobbing around the room like a pinball. She was throwing yesterday's clothes into her bag and frantically grabbing at her makeup from the bathroom sink.

"Anna, slow down," Mary prodded gently. "Just hang on," Anna stopped, about to toss a tube of mascara in. Her eyes were a little wild.

"Are you sure you want to leave?"

"Mary," Anna took a breath, dropped the tube in the bag and plopped down on the bed. "I have wanted to leave since I got here," her face crumpled a bit.

"What are you talking about? Why?"

"I know that Kurt is the official creator of FantasyCoin, but it's *my* life. My baby. I was never comfortable with all of us coming here and leaving it alone, but I didn't want to admit it. And," she looked down at her hands. "You're doing fine."

"What is that supposed to mean?" Consternation spread over Mary's face.

"The *only* reason I pitched the Wood Smoke Lodge to Kurt was because I thought you were in trouble. You talk to me like you're going broke, like you're about to lose the lodge. You say you can't stand dealing with Mom anymore. You seem lonely. But, then I get here, and here you are, looking amazing. Keeping the Lodge in tip-top shape despite the slow business. And then to watch you and Kurt flirt with each other? It's like, I wanna vomit or something," Anna let out a self-conscious laugh. Mary joined in.

"Are you going to be okay with it? Are you going to be okay leaving?"

"It's more than Kurt, Mare. I need this. I need to get away and regroup. Let you and Kurt do your thing. Let the rest of the company enjoy their trip. I'm just going to be a drag," Anna smiled in spite of herself. Mary eased down onto the bed and beside her sister.

"I love you," she whispered as she wrapped her arms around Anna's broad shoulders.

"Love you, too," Anna whispered back, hooking her hands onto Mary's arms. "I gotta go. Fantasy needs me," she gently pushed Mary back and her smiled turned to a smirk. "Or should I say, *reality* needs me?"

Mary fake punched her in the arm and stood. "You're a nerd. Give me your bag, and I'll go put it in the car."

Mary took Anna's bag, zipped it for her, and trotted down the staircase. Everyone but Kurt was sitting in the great room.

Mary overheard Rory and Kato discussing the server issues. Unable to translate it, she broke into the conversation politely. "Excuse me, guys. Anyone know where Kurt is? I need to put this in his car."

"He went out there to warm it up for Anna," Maci replied.

Mary's heart leapt into her throat for a quick beat, and she pushed her way out the front door and into the cold morning.

She wrapped her arms around herself, tucked her chin down, and headed out through the falling flurries and to the modest parking lot, where her jeep and the three cars set, now a couple inches into the snow. Kurt was at the windshield, wiping the accumulated snow off the glass with the sleeve of his ski jacket.

As Mary made her way toward the humming sedan, Kurt looked out at her, his eyes squinting under his knit hat.

"I have no idea what I'm doing," he laughed.

"You're doing great." Mary returned his laugh.

He stepped around and took the bag from her, and his gloved hand gripped her bare fingers. She hesitated to let go, but he hefted it away from her and opened the trunk, tucking the bag securely inside.

"You must be freezing. Here." He rubbed her arms roughly before blanketing her shoulders with his own arm and gently directing her back to the deck. Mary's blood rushed to every tip in her body- her fingers, her head, her ears. She felt light-headed and wanted to collapse into Kurt. As they summited the deck, Anna emerged from the front door, apparently ready. Kurt and Mary parted.

"I'm out of here. I'll handle everything. Don't you worry, boss." Mary noticed that Anna looked more chipper than she had the whole time she'd been there.

"I trust you, Anna. And, thank you. Truly." He patted her on the shoulder and began to walk her to the car.

"Drive safe, Ann," Mary called after her as Anna picked her way down the icy steps. Mary watched Kurt opened the door for her, say something, and then step back from the car. Anna closed the door and set the car in reverse. Kurt moved around it and started back toward the deck.

Instead of pulling out right away, Anna unrolled the passenger side window.

"Take care of my sister, Kurt!" She called from within the warm car. Kurt pivoted around, and waved back at her.

"Take care of our company, Anna."

# Chapter 41

Kurt stomped each foot as he climbed the short staircase up onto the deck.

"Thank you for that," Mary commented to him, warmly.

"No. Thank your sister. Without her, FantasyCoin wouldn't be what it is. I wish the server hadn't crashed. I wish she would stay. But, I think that she really did want to leave."

"She did." Mary confirmed and moved to go inside. "Trust me."

As they entered the lodge, the warmer air blasted them. The others seemed to be growing a little anxious.

"What's up with the servers, boss?" Eddie asked as he paced back and forth in front of the fire place.

"All is well. Anna is on the job. She wanted to get out of here. A little cabin fever, I think. We are ready to embrace the retreat now. I give you all permission to stop worrying about FantasyCoin," Kurt waved his hand in front of them as if to wipe away their frowns.

Maci, however, was already grinning ear to ear.

"Alright, Mary. Rumor has it we are literally going to chop down trees. Is this true?" Maci was shaking with excitement.

"Well," Mary broke into a grin, "the rumor is true, actually. But, I did not take you for a tree-choppin' kind of girl, Maci. I'm so glad you're excited," Mary stepped over behind the reception desk as Maci chattered on about how she, herself, wouldn't be doing any chopping, but she was excited to be part of the experience.

"Okay, everyone!" Mary called out as she dragged a box over. "Welcome to the official Wood Smoke Retreat on Maplewood Mountain. I'd like to inform you that FantasyCoin actually gets to experience the first ever team-building retreat program in all of Maplewood. First of its kind!" She raised her voice to imitate the ring leader of a circus.

Kurt loved it. He moved back toward the sofa and leaned against it, taking a quick inventory of his employees and noting their reactions to Mary's adorable directions.

They all listened intently as Mary described the competition. They were to break up into teams. Each team was given a handsaw and a tarp and was instructed to go into the woods, find a worthy Christmas tree, and return it to the lodge, unscathed. The team with the prettiest tree won the competition and got a beautiful, forest-themed prize basket. The trees would be decorated and posted up in the lodge with little placards heralding their origins.

Kurt felt like a little boy again. He couldn't remember the last time he'd participated in a silly game. Or any game, really. He loved Mary's idea and saw that the incentive had piqued everyone's interest.

Mary pulled out three hand saws and three bow saws, setting each on the hearth.

"Alright, everyone. Let's break into teams. Three groups would be ideal, which means, let's see," Mary did a quick head count. "Seven of you. That makes one group of three and one of four. Although," she paused thinking over her options. "Four gives one team and unfair advantage."

Kurt jumped in. "I've got an idea. I'll work with Mary. We'll be the home team," he pushed off from the sofa and strode over to stand next to her. He caught Maci roll her eyes and smile. "Is that fair?"

Everyone nodded in agreement. Maci, Alex, and Jace teamed up. Eddie, Kato, and Rory. Mary and Kurt. They grabbed their saws and set off through the back door, down the steps and into the snowy woods as some of them pulled hats and hoods over their heads and zipped their down jackets and coats. The snow had stopped, but the sky was still heavy with the threat of more.

Right away, Alex and Rory took charge over their teams, barking out orders and scrambling through the high snow.

"Be safe out there!" Mary called ahead of her as the two groups disappeared into the trees.

Kurt adjusted his gloves, rubbed his hands together, and took Mary's shoulders in his hands. "Alright, Innkeeper," he started as he searched Mary's green irises.

He seemed to lose himself for a moment. Mary raised her left eyebrow and bit her lower lip. Kurt inhaled and let out a puff of frosty air. "Do you know of any secret places? I want to win."

# Chapter 42

As they shuffled through the snow, Mary's stomach twisted into knots. She snuggled her hands into her scarlet-red down jacket as a shiver coursed through her body. Kurt must have mistaken her nerves for a chill, because he moved closer to her as they made their way through scrubby pine trees and snow-covered oak saplings. Their arms brushed each other, his ski jacket swishing against her coat. The pair trekked together silently into the woods, nothing escaping their lips but icy exhalations.

Before long, the other two groups were out of sight. Wood Smoke's property spanned many acres, but surely none of them had walked too far.

Still, the combination of the heavy snow and thick trees quickly blurred their sight lines.

Mary pointed up and to the left, her hand cutting in front of Kurt's chest. "I think there is a little clearing that way with some fallen fir trees. We could see if there are any younger firs that look nice and plump?" She looked up at him beneath the faux fur-lined hood of her coat, pushing it up a bit with her hand.

He smiled down at her.

"Perfect," he replied, as he grabbed her mitten hand. It startled her, and she began to lean away, creating resistance against his pull.

He began to turn to her, but then she gripped his hand more firmly and tucked herself nearer to him. Kurt grinned again at her, and she noticed, maybe for the first time, how smooth his lips were as he wiped a bit of frost from his beard.

She considered slipping her mitten off to feel the same smoothness in his hand, but thought better of it.

Mary still wasn't sold on Kurt's city life and office work. Even the duds she had dated opened her doors with calloused hands and rough knuckles. She liked that. What would her dad think of soft hands on a man?

She shook her head, clearing the thought away. How silly it was for her to even make the leap that Kurt would ever meet Mr. Delaney. Laughable really.

"Everything okay?" Kurt hugged her closer to him and looked down at her.

Mary flushed. "Yes, yes. Sorry, I was just thinking to myself. It's nothing." She shook her head again and looked down into the fresh snow as her boots squashed into its clean surface.

They came upon the clearing just then. Kurt stopped and turned to her.

"What were you thinking? I'd love to know," he pulled her other hand into his, swiveled to face her, and marched them backward together a few paces until they reached a fallen log. Kurt tugged her down onto it next to him. She had the urge to fall with him into the snow and cover his mouth with hers.

But, she resisted.

"Oh, really. It's nothing," she grinned to herself and dipped her head. He let go of one hand, forcing her to jerk her head back up in question.

"I have to be honest, I'm not sure how you and I will manage this together, especially without a saw," his mouth curled up on one side and Mary's hand flew to her mouth.

"Oh no! I left ours on the deck. Ugh, we'll have to go back. I'm so sorry," she began to push up from the log, but Kurt pulled her back down more roughly than before and took her face in his hands.

He looked at her for a moment then pushed her hood back from her face. A strand of her hair slipped out over her ear. Mary brought her hand up to brush it away, but he beat her to it, tucking the hair neatly behind her ear.

Her hand fell to his wrist, and her breath caught in her throat. She felt her chest rising and falling in shallow heaves. Kurt began to lean his face in closer when suddenly they heard the crack of a branch.

Mary shot up from the log, practically knocking Kurt off. Eddie was not ten yards off, moving toward them. He was whacking a long, thick stick against tree trunks as he made his way.

Mary heard Kurt sigh below her and felt him rise up.

"Eddie, what's up?" Kurt called over, a slight edge to his voice.

Eddie finally focused on them, oblivious to what they were doing. Or, rather, about to do.

"Guys, I am totally lost. Thank God I found you. Kato and Rory sent me back to get drinks. I think this is going to take us a while. Well, now it definitely will, because I have no idea which direction to walk in to get back to the deck." Eddie whacked another trunk.

"We can walk you back," Mary replied at the same time as Kurt.

"We have to go get our saw anyway." Kurt's voice had softened and he stuffed his hands into his own jacket pockets.

Mary felt a shard of disappointment cut into her ribs when Kurt agreed that they'd better go back. She wished they would just shoo Eddie away so Kurt could take her face back into his hands and press his mouth onto hers. She ached with a longing that had been suppressed for months. Years, even. And now there was no more hiding it away, tucking it neatly into a dusty drawer.

"Let's hurry so we don't lose much time," Mary urged. The trio took off in the direction of the lodge, Mary leading the way.

# Chapter 43

In fewer than five minutes, they had descended upon the snow-encrusted Lodge.

Eddie trudged past them, muttering under his breath about the cold. Once Eddie was safely indoors, Kurt began to move around Mary to get to the deck. He was close enough behind her, that he couldn't help but let his hand trail across her lower back. He felt her arch her back slightly, and he had to still himself before mounting the steps.

Mary busied herself by clearing the charred, sodden logs from the pit and setting them off to the side.

"Are we having another fireside tonight?" He asked as he trotted back down the steps, saw in hand.

"It's up to the group. We might all be a little too frost-bitten by then."

"Hang on a sec," he stopped, pretending to be suspicious, "Just how long are you keeping us in the woods?"

Mary laughed and kicked a clump of snow at him. It sprayed over his legs, and he was tempted to kick back but thought better of it.

"I'd be careful if I were you," he cautioned, shaking his gloved finger at her, mockingly.

"Oh? And why's that. Are you the abominable snowman?"

He chuckled at her cheesy joke and started to reach out to goose her in the ribs, but the sound of the door opening behind them stopped him. He quickly let his hand fall.

"Got the goods, Ed?" Kurt called up. Eddie stumbled down the slippery steps with a couple beer cans he must have rooted out of the fridge.

"Ready to roll, boss. Mary, hope it's okay that I found these?"

"Absolutely. That's what I have them for, after all. I am not a big drinker. Oh, and Eddie? Will you be able to find your way to your group?"

"No, probably not. I was counting on blind luck, really."

Kurt could tell that Eddie noticed the significant pause between the three of them. Mary looked to Kurt, her face pinched in worry. She bit down on her lip, chewing at it gently.

"Well," Kurt started, tucking the saw, blade-side down, under his arm. He rubbed his hands together to generate some heat. Kurt considered for a moment what to do. Agree to walk Eddie back and lose out on time to cut a tree and, more importantly, alone time with Mary? Send Eddie off into the blanketed woods without help? Kurt sniffed and shifted his weight, before finishing his response. "I'll go ahead and…"

"I'll be fine, actually," Eddie interrupted suddenly. Kurt made eye contact with him and saw Eddie break into a subtle smile.

"Oh, we should really go with you," Mary broke in.

"No, no, no. I will carry some twigs and pebbles and leave a trail of breadcrumbs for myself. It wouldn't be fair to force a time disadvantage on you. There are only two of you as it is. You need every bit of help you can get."

And then, before Kurt could respond, he caught Eddie wink at him. "I'm serious. You go. I'll be fine. I promise. If you don't find me by lunch, send out the dogs."

And with that, Eddie launched off back into the snow, bending down with every couple strides to pick up debris to use as his proverbial breadcrumbs.

Kurt redirected his gaze down to Mary, who was now watching Eddie embark into the white beyond while she continued teething her lip. Her arms were crossed over her chest. She didn't look up.

"He'll be fine," Kurt assured her. He knew Eddie was a goofball who might've gotten lost initially, but he wasn't worried. He could tell Mary was.

She dropped her arms and clapped bits of bark and frost from her hands and knees.

"If you're sure," she said as smiled up at him, shrugged her coat down a bit, and started back off into the woods.

"Mary, wait," he called ahead.

She stopped and turned in her little burrow of snow. A mischievous look crossed her face for a moment before her eyebrows settled into their perfect arches and she waited for him to speak.

136

"Maybe you and I should stay here. Keep the home fires burning. Wait it out… just in case?"

"No way, Kurt Cutler. We have a tree to chop down." And with that, she turned back into the woods and stomped through snow that was nearly to her knees. She was way ahead of him, and he knew it.

# Chapter 44

All Mary wanted to do was cuddle up on the sofa in front of a fire. It sounded safe. And Mary definitely wanted to cuddle with Kurt Cutler. But first, she had to test him.

She started her way back to the clearing, and her prior notions of kissing on the log had evaporated.

Now, she wanted to see him in action. Could a city boy with smooth hands hack it? Because if not, then where could this flirtation even go?

Nowhere. Mary was not Anna. She wouldn't let herself get swept up in a weekend love spree. She wanted something lasting. Didn't most women? If Anna was the exception, Mary was the rule. Steadfast. Sure-footed.

Mary often thought about Anna. Worried about her. What was her sister looking for? What was she so intent to avoid? Why? They had the exact same upbringing. And yet, two of the four of them had largely followed in their mother's footsteps (or, at least, Mary *planned* to).

Then there was Anna. And Roberta. Complete opposites of Erica and Mary. Unreliable, wild, and boy crazy. And yet, the four of them were sisters through and through. They loved each other with a loyalty that got them into trouble sometimes.

Just as Mary was starting to fall further into thought, Kurt caught her arm and whipped her around.

"I can't wait," Kurt sputtered, breathlessly.

Mary looked up at him, critically, as he gripped her arms. She wasn't sure if he meant wait to go inside or wait for the exact same thing she was waiting for.

But she had come to a realization. She needed to see him first. Watching him give up on walking Eddie back to the others and limply carry the saw hadn't impressed her. She needed to know him. Before she could kiss him.

Mary moved into Kurt's arms, pulling her body to his. She placed her hands on his shoulders and pressed herself up closer to his face. He lowered to reach her in hungry anticipation.

But Mary pressed her cheek against his, feeling just how cold he was, and whispered into his ear.

"You'll have to." She lowered herself back down, sliding one hand along his jacket. He lilted backward, but caught her hand in his and let her pull him for a step or two.

Dropping his hand, she forged ahead. This time, instead of the clearing, she guided him to a hotspot of the fullest, most beautiful fir trees on the property. Mary had a new goal now.

"We aren't going back to where we were?"

"I know of a better place. Better trees."

Kurt groaned quietly. But he followed her, and soon enough they'd landed at the little fir grove.

"We might even win the competition," Mary uttered as she started weaving between the fir trees and scattered spruces.

"You know what? We should maybe pick a blue spruce instead. They are so beautiful," she suggested while combing up the branches of an especially plump, tall spruce.

She didn't hear Kurt reply, so she looked back over her shoulder. His arms were crossed over his chest, but he had one hand covering his mouth as though he was stifling a laugh. His eyes crinkled at the corners, and Mary saw what it was when someone really and truly smiled with their eyes.

She grinned back and tugged the corners of her hood over her ears. "What? Why are you smiling like that?"

"You're adorable, Mary Delaney."

Mary felt her cheeks grow hot. She bit down on her lip and rolled her eyes, trying to throw off the heat.

"I had no idea there were different kinds of Christmas trees," he continued, moving in on her, the saw bobbing under his arm still.

"Men!" She threw up her hands in mock exasperation. And she turned back around, about to start in on explaining what to do, despite the fact that she, herself, had never ever cut down a tree.

139

Mary heard something fall into the powdery snow and then felt Kurt's hands begin to creep around her puffy coat in a hug. This would be harder than she realized. And not just for Kurt.

Mary was dying to feel his lips on her. Still, she needed to see him in the light in which she had seen every other Maplewood man. Every other *real* man. Was Kurt more than a computer and backup servers?

# Chapter 45

She covered his hands with hers and peeled them off of her.

"Get to work," she cooed in a sing-song voice.

He literally could not keep his hands off of her. But this time, he dropped them and bent down to retrieve the wet saw. She raised an eyebrow at it, and he picked up on her hint. Wiping the thin blade of the saw across his jeans, he stood back and measured the tree with his eyes.

"Obviously, I have never done this," he started. "But, I am more than up to the task. Mary, I'm about to win you the prize basket," he joked. Mary laughed and hugged herself to keep warm before standing back as if to watch a show.

"You sure all I need is a bow saw? Shouldn't we have a hatchet or ax to cut a notch first?" He scratched his head through his beanie, thinking through the process.

"My dad and brothers use just the saw and get it done in no time." She hid a smirk with her mittened hand, but he could see the dare in her eyes.

It was effective. Kurt bent down and tried to fit his broad shoulders beneath the lowest boughs, but the tree wasn't that big, and he stuck out halfway.

He felt her watch him as he began to saw, moving the blade forward and back rhythmically. He gained momentum and fell into a seesaw pattern for leverage.

Mary wished she had thought to bring a thermos of cocoa or a blanket. She had the distinct urge to massage his shoulders or even cheer as he went, but that sounded silly in reality. So, she resisted and instead called out words of encouragement here and there.

It seemed fewer than five minutes before he stood up and let the bow fall to his side. With his free hand, he pulled his beanie from his head and shoved it into his jacket pocket.

Mary squatted down to see what he'd done. She was impressed. He made a notch after all.

"Nice work, Paul Bunyan." She teased.

"Stand a little ways behind me, just in case I've miscalculated." He commanded. She did as she was told, trudging over to him and beyond by a few paces.

Kurt knelt back down and moved the saw to the other side. He pumped hard for a longer period of time, taking few breaks.

Before long, Kurt shot back and up from under the tree.

"Timber!" He cried out. The blue branches quivered for a moment before the massive thing collapsed into the snow.

Kurt turned to Mary, a triumphant look spreading across his handsome face. He looked at her, pointedly.

"You must work out," she smiled back and took a couple steps back toward him, her boots heavy with snow and ice. "Do you lift weights? I can picture you back down in the valley. Maybe in some clean warehouse of a gym where everyone struts around with earbuds, giving off a 'don't look at me, but look at me' vibe." She paused for effect. It worked.

"You got me there," he outstretched his hand to her, helping her wade through the last couple snowy feet.

They sunk together into the chunky snow that kissed at the frosty felled tree.

"But I don't usually have a partner during my workouts. That'll have to change today. Do you have it in you to help me haul this? Or, are you going to stand back and watch some more?"

He felt a distinct shift in their relationship right then. It went from uncertain tension to comfortable flirting. It warmed him a bit, despite the frigid air.

"Let's do it," she nodded her head and moved to the top of the tree. Though it hadn't snowed the whole time they were out there, it felt as though the snow was deepening around them.

Kurt remembered when he would ski as a teenager, the same thing would happen after a full day on the slopes. It would become harder and harder to trudge out of a ditch.

All he wanted to do was pull Mary down into the snow with him and kiss her. But he had read her loud and clear.

He needed to pass her test.

# Chapter 46

Each of the groups had made it back to the lodge ahead of Mary and Kurt. Even Eddie was there, rubbing his hands vigorously in front of the fire and shivering out of control.

Mary wondered if he had gotten lost after all.

Each group had rested their trees on the back deck, letting the snow and ice drip through the wooden planks. When Mary and Kurt joined the others inside, she turned her innkeeper persona back on.

"Wow, everyone! I'm so impressed with your hard work. It's lunchtime, so I think we'll go ahead and let the trees dry out a little before we commence the judging. Feel free to get changed or wash up for lunch. I've got yummy potpies waiting to be baked."

Everyone, including Kurt, headed up the stairs. Mary had shrugged out of her coat and boots at the back deck, but her feet were numb. She put off changing out her socks until she preheated the oven and set water to boil for tea. Once she was in the kitchen, she figured she'd set the table, too.

Not ten minutes later, the others were streaming down the stairs in a hurry for lunch. She made her way past them calling that she'd be back in a pinch.

Kurt wasn't part of the group. *He must still be in his room*, Mary thought. She paused at his door, but when she couldn't hear him rustling around, she moved on and into her own room.

Once there, she changed out of her snow socks and into some cozy sheepskin slippers that Erica had sent her a few years ago.

Before she headed back downstairs, she checked her phone and noticed a text from Anna.

*Halfway point. Don't worry about me- I'm glad I left. Feeling better already.*

Mary smiled and tapped out a quick reply.

*Good. Love you so much. Text/call when you make it to town.*

She pocketed the phone and strode out of the room and back down the stairs, peering over the banister and into the dining room. There was Kurt, at his spot along the far end of the bench, next to Maci this time. It seemed everyone else had sort of played musical chairs, except for him.

As she ducked into the kitchen, she quickly transferred the pies onto two pans and into the oven.

Then, she pulled the loaf of cornbread from the pantry. She had bought the potpies and cornbread from Leslie's beforehand and felt a little guilty. At least it wasn't grocery-store-bought, she assured herself.

She wrenched the bread from its plastic sleeve and set about slicing it and situating it onto a pretty Christmas tree plate.

She finished the tea and took the pitcher and plate to the waiting guests, who devoured the bread and chugged the iced tea greedily.

The rest of lunch was a chatty affair, with each group regaling the others with the tale of how they manage to fell their Christmas trees with such "primitive" tools.

Mary enjoyed listening in on their banter as she dished out the pot pies, cleared plates here and there and managed to steal a few bites of her own in the kitchen.

During one such occasion, Kurt peeked in on her, catching her as she slid a forkful of pie into her mouth. She pressed her lips down over the utensil to prevent crumbs from slipping through the tines.

They locked eyes. She chewed for a moment and then covered her mouth as she swallowed and mumbled a "Sorry," embarrassed.

"Sorry for eating? You're crazy. Why don't you eat with us?" He asked, fully entering the kitchen.

"Not how I run things here. I like guests to be comfortable, but it would be awkward for me to have to excuse myself from the table regularly to check on things, tidy things, refill glasses, and so on. I think you forgot that I'm the official hostess and acting in an official capacity," she pointed out.

"Touché," he replied. "I guess I see you in a different light."

"I'm going to get things cleaned up, and then we will judge the trees. But," she paused, her eyebrows furrowing as she focused off into the great room. "How can I be an unbiased judge? I didn't think this through very well."

"I think I have an idea, actually," he scratched his beard. "Eddie. Didn't you hear? He ended up getting lost again. It was miraculous that he made it back here just as the others were depositing their trees on the deck."

Mary laughed loudly. She couldn't help it.

"What's so funny in here?" It was Maci, stepping into the kitchen like a quiet little mouse.

"I heard about Eddie," Mary replied.

"Oh, I know! I felt so terrible for him! The poor guy," Maci pouted and moved toward the sink, where she unloaded her glass and plate. "That was super scrumptious, Mary. You are the best cook ever."

Mary nodded her head and smiled, refusing to reveal the truth of her indiscretion.

She wiped her hands on a nearby dishtowel and then passed between Kurt and Maci and into the dining room.

She didn't want to give Maci too much to work with. She was learning quickly that Maci was a meddler. Mary didn't mind so much, but she did not want to answer any nosey questions.

"Alright, lumbermen... and woman," she looked back over her shoulder as Kurt and Maci followed her to the table.

The chatter at the table stalled and the others looked up at her. "It's judgment time," she beamed at the frost-bitten crew of tired computer nerds.

A moment of worry passed through her as she thought maybe the so-called team-building activity missed the mark or was a little *too* hard.

But then Jace, inexplicably, started a chant.

"We *win*! We *win*!" He carried on as the others whooped and playfully swatted at him.

Mary's smile returned. Relieved she clapped twice.

"Because of a serious conflict of interest," she started, provoking their interest. Jace and Kato exchanged a knowing glance, and Mary could feel Maci rile as though a scandal was about to be revealed. "I, your fearless leader- at least, for this retreat- cannot be the judge. The good news is," she waited, stirring their anticipation, "it came to my attention that Eddie got lost again after his initial detour!"

The room broke into laughter, Eddie included. Rory stood up and rounded behind Eddie, squeezing his shoulders and rocking him side to side roughly.

"Eddie, you idiot!" Kato cried out, collapsing into another round of laughs.

"He's not an idiot," Maci corrected, defensively. "It was really hard to get around out there." Her pout returned and Mary offered her a sympathetic look.

"Whatever the excuse," Mary continued, both taming and encouraging the ridicule that showered over poor Eddie. "I am assigning Eddie as the one-and-only, first-ever Christmas Tree Judge at Wood Smoke Lodge!" Mary's voice rose in excitement and the group cheered wildly.

She looked back at Kurt, who clapped along and nodded to her, a slow grin creeping behind his beard.

# Chapter 47

The rest of the afternoon descended upon them like a blur. Everyone was exhausted. Eddie stole the show during the tree judging, naming his own group as the winner, despite cries from everyone else that he was supposed to be unbiased.

Kurt observed as Mary guided the others in propping their trees into the tree stands she had acquired just for this weekend.

She next dragged over two bins filled with twinkle lights and glass ornaments and one with wooden and metal ornaments. Her organization was impressive.

Mary was an expert at making men work for her; this Kurt had realized much earlier, of course.

Kato and Alex positioned one of the trees by the reception desk, one in the great room, and one behind the old farm table dining room, partially blocking the bay window.

Mary draped oversized tree skirts under each tree and directed the teams to spread out in decorating them as she put on what Kurt realized was probably the only CD she owned- the Christmas music one.

Kurt offered to help Mary, and so she shooed him to go string the lights and mount the stars atop each tree. He did as he was told, and Mary excused herself again to the kitchen to prepare some more hot cocoa as the groups toiled away.

Kurt had never enjoyed himself this much. And it blew his mind. He hadn't even thought about his phone. Back at home, he was glued to it. It was practically the most important thing in his life. Next to his job. And his computer. And every other thing that was so opposite to life on the mountain.

Of course, he hadn't explored Maplewood much, but even being tucked away at Wood Smoke didn't feel as suffocating as he thought it might.

This was a real weekend. A real retreat. Getting away from it all. Being outside, even in the freezing temps. Huddling around a fire as Eddie thawed out. Even the group was having a blast.

The tree trimming came to a close, and the group sipped the rest of their hot cocoas as they stood back, admiring their hard work.

Rory was particularly skilled at decorating. He managed to get Kato and Alex to balance the ornaments so beautifully that the great room spruce looked like it could be photographed for a catalog.

"I'm literally wiped out," Maci complained, slumping into the love seat next to Eddie, who was still acting like he might have some sort of long-lasting physical trauma.

"Me, too," Mary plopped down onto the hearth and yawned. Kurt studied her, looking for hints but finding nothing but heavy eyelids. She flipped her hair over her head, and his knees felt weak.

"I vote for a break," Eddie chimed in. The others nodded.

Kurt checked his watch. It was already almost four.

"What time is dinner, Mary?" He asked her as the others started to fade out of consciousness already.

"Well, I put on a pot roast while we were enjoying lunch. It should be ready no later than six, and we'll want to start it by that time so it doesn't dry out," Mary yawned again. Kurt wondered if a sleepless night was catching up to her, too. He, himself, stifled a yawn.

"Let's say quarter to six?" Alex suggested as he stood. "I'm not that tired. I'm sure we can all manage to hang in there?"

"Five thirty, how about? Enough time for you to sneak in a cat nap or unwind a bit in your room. You're also welcome to set up a board game or hang out on the deck. I think the fire pit is clear enough to start up another fire now if you think you'll be too tired after dinner?" Mary offered.

The group mumbled affirmations and nodded their heads.

"Sounds good to me. Great work today everyone!" Kurt interjected as they started to stand and part ways. Alex, Rory, Kato, and Jace decided to enjoy the remainder of last night's cigars on the deck, excluding Eddie, who decided to take a hot bath.

Mary and Kurt remained in the great room- Mary on the hearth, still. Kurt rounded the sofa and joined her.

He noticed Mary's eyes following Maci as she tapped her phone all the way up the stairs.

"So Maci has a boyfriend back home?" She asked.

"Truth be told, I know very little about the team's personal lives. I try to keep things as separate as possible. But Maci is an open-book. She and her boyfriend are very on-again, off-again. In fact, I'm not convinced that it's a," he searched for the right word. "A committed relationship," he finished.

He looked at Mary, who seemed to be considering his information. His lips parted as he was about to go on, but she cut in.

"I have to wonder just how much of your team actually believes in committed relationships. I know Anna doesn't," she glanced at him then rested her eyes on the coffee table. He thought he saw a flush creep up her face. Maybe she was embarrassed for asking the question, but he appreciated her honesty.

"Well, maybe not Maci. Or Anna. Or any of them. But," he shifted his weight, bracing his hands on his knees, nervously. "I do."

# Chapter 48

Mary silently cursed herself for passing judgment on the FantasyCoin Team. It was rude and unbecoming. So, when Kurt flipped the question like that, she felt she was nearing some sort of answer to something.

Kurt's suggestion was obvious, but Mary still didn't want to believe it. This weekend had felt like a whirlwind- between having a packed house at the Lodge and meeting this guy who was equal parts incredibly attractive and incredibly not her type, Mary felt torn. Undoubtedly, she wanted to fall into Kurt's arms and live happily ever after.

But then, she wasn't a naïve teenager. She worried how this might end: Kurt going back to the city and allowing his work and beautiful big-city girls to remind him why he lived there; Mary, in Maplewood, with a broken heart.

She stood, abruptly. "I forgot. I haven't prepped the cookie dough and brownie batter for tonight's dessert." It was true. It was the one thing Mary hadn't at least somewhat prepared for the weekend. She had simply run out of time.

Kurt joined her in standing. Maybe he could read her hesitation. She hoped, however, that he wasn't giving up. She didn't want him to give up.

"I'd love your help?" She asked him, allowing herself a small smile.

"I'd love *to* help," he returned her smile and stiffly thrust his hands into his jean pockets. But, ah, do we have time for a quick shower?" He looked a little sheepish. But, he had a point. They all still needed to thaw out a bit and freshen up.

"Actually, that's a great idea. In fact, I'm going to join you," she caught herself. Kurt's eyebrows shot up and he leaned back. "Oops! I meant..." They laughed in unison. "I meant that I'm going to take a shower, too."

Forty-five minutes later, they had both emerged and met up in the kitchen. Mary felt more relaxed and open. She only had about half an hour left, so she took full advantage of Kurt, directing him here and there- to grab this jar and that package from the pantry.

She pulled the bowls and pans and preheated the oven. They worked in tandem like a pair of synchronized swimmers. Kurt seemed to know his way around the kitchen, which intrigued Mary.

She had him read off the recipe to her. She scooped and sprinkled, stirred and wiped her hands on the little red apron she'd thrown on.

Once both batters were done, she held up a teaspoonful of cookie dough for Kurt's approval. He tasted it, his eyes lighting up.

"Delicious," he confirmed and licked his lips and reached behind her for a clean ladle from the counter. "Your turn."

He dipped the ladle into the brownie batter and held his hand under it to catch chocolatey drips and then offered it to her lips.

Awkwardly, she opened her mouth, hardly wide enough for the wooden spoon. Kurt laughed as she tried to test the batter. Chocolate made its way all the way up one of her cheeks. She put her hand up to wipe it, but Kurt beat her and gently cleared it, taking the bit of batter into his own mouth.

"Also delicious," he grinned. Mary's stomach flipped. Shifting their focus, but only barely, she began to butter the cookie sheets and brownie pan. Kurt jumped in instantly, scooping spoons of dough onto the sheets, almost perfectly.

"Have you done this before?" She wondered aloud.

"Not really," he replied.

"Did your mom bake a lot? You seem... practiced," Mary laughed.

"Definitely not. Or if she did, it was never in front of me."

Mary was curious. Gently, she asked him to go on. Over the next ten minutes, Kurt told her about his upbringing. He never wanted for anything from her parents. Except affection. Sometimes even love.

Mary couldn't tell if she felt bad for the little boy who Kurt once was. She could picture him, in a grand playroom in a mansion-sized, ranch-style house in the valley, surrounded by toys and gadgets. Televisions, DVD players. Computers. His parents not around. It was definitely different than her own experience. But maybe not too different.

"We had very little when we were younger. In fact, I don't remember having hardly any toys. Just a few hand-sewn dolls that had belonged to my sisters. We spent all our time with our parents while we worked alongside them on the farm."

"That sounds hard," he replied, spooning the last of the dough onto the second sheet.

"It was," Mary finished scraping the last of the batter into the pan. "But, we had a lot of love. Hugs and kisses. All of us."

"Yeah, you have quite a few siblings, don't you?"

"That's right. Two brothers and three sisters. I'm the youngest girl."

Just then, Maci and Eddie bobbed their way down the stairs, in front of the rest of the team. Mary was amazed at how they all seemed to move in a pack.

Dinner went similarly to lunch, except everyone seemed a little better rested. Before long, Mary was cleaning up the last of the dishes, and the team was arranging themselves in the living room with their little dessert plates. Kurt had asked them to hang around for a few moments so he could have at least one formal little meeting.

Mary continued cleaning the kitchen, but she listened in on his lecture. He was congratulating them on a great year, making sure to note at least one specific thing each person had contributed to FantasyCoin's success.

She could hear him applaud Eddie's positivity and fun spirit and Kato's razor-sharp focus. After getting through every single team member, he finally came to her sister.

"And we can't forget about Anna. Anna is really the one who runs this company. She is the heart and soul. So much so that she was willing to head back down and handle the server issue."

His praise yielded another little round of applause, just as the other compliments had.

Hearing that, Mary neatly folded up the last of the little stack of clean dishtowels. She had found the answer she was looking for.

# Chapter 49

As became a sort of pattern, the guys took to the back deck to shoot the breeze. Maci, of course, was too tired and instead climbed the staircase at just before seven o'clock.

Kurt joined Mary in the kitchen once he'd finished talking with the group. She was standing at the counter pre-setting the coffee maker. He noticed how she looked in her worn jeans and easy sweatshirt. She looked like someone he wanted to hug and never let go.

"Are you thinking of joining the guys outside?" She asked as she turned to face him.

"No. Mary, I need to talk to you." Kurt's stern tone gave her pause, but she nodded her head and crossed her arms in front of her chest.

"Can we go anywhere... private?"

"Unfortunately, I think the most private place, apart from our rooms, is right here," Mary replied, indicating the kitchen, dining room, great room, and reception area in one sweep of her delicate hand.

Kurt seemed to consider it for a moment. When he didn't immediately reply, Mary offered an alternative.

"We could bundle up and go for another chilly walk in the woods?" A devilish grin curled across her mouth. Unsmiling, Kurt dipped his head.

"If you're game, I am," he said, crossing his arms as if to challenge her. His anxiety waned somewhat.

"Yeah, sure," Mary didn't hesitate for long and brushed past him toward the coat rack at the back door.

Tension curtailed their flirtation from earlier.

Kurt followed her. They pulled on their jackets and then doubled back to the hearth where they grabbed their boots, sat, and stuffed their feet into them, working silently alongside each other.

Finally, they strolled back to the front door. Kurt stole a furtive glance back behind them as he opened the door for Mary. His nerves kicked back up. He was about to risk a lot.

They were met with a cold, still air. Slowly, their eyes adapted to the black night. No stars or moon lit their way, but Mary had grabbed an old-fashioned lantern from the front closet. It provided just barely enough light for them to see about two steps ahead.

They hesitated together, noiselessly, at the edge of the deck and seemed to both admire the darkness before them. The few cars in the modest little parking lot peeked out from the snow, almost imperceptibly, like hibernating bears. The nearby highway was completely invisible to them. They had complete privacy.

Kurt offered to take the lamp, and Mary let him. Neither of them had put on their gloves. Everyone's gloves were baking on the hearth.

As they perched on the lip of the top step, Kurt extended his free hand, palm up, out in front of Mary.

She seemed to consider it for a moment before she took it, not looking up at him.

He guided her as they gingerly moved down the steps and farther into the icy night air.

Kurt knew he was the one who initiated the private talk, but he couldn't quite find the words. He felt Mary's hand grow a little cold in his, and he pulled through his arm and to his chest.

Mary was the one to speak up first.

"I was really impressed that you included Anna in your little speech. She wasn't here. You didn't need to do that."

"What? Oh, well, of course, I included her. I meant what I said. Your sister is very good at her job."

"Is it weird to you that she was sort of, uh, struggling with this?" Mary waved her hand in a circle between them.

Kurt answered right away. "Not at all. I think it was professional of her to be a little uncomfortable. She was trying to keep things above board for everyone, I think."

Mary didn't reply. Kurt slowed his pace.

"Listen, Mary. I know we have only known each other all of two days. Not even." Kurt slowed down more. They had just made it past the parking lot and into the woods that framed that side of the property.

"It feels like longer," Mary stopped and peeked up at him from under her fluffy hood. Kurt stopped and faced her.

155

"Yeah, you're right." He felt compelled to pull her closer to him, mushing her puffy coat into his jacket. She was quite a bit smaller than he, so he ducked his head down and leaned back a little to meet her eyes.

"Mary, I really like you. A lot."

There. He said it.

He studied her as her eyebrows wrinkled for a moment and then softened. The corners of her lips upturned and her mouth parted as she began to respond.

"I like you, too, Kurt." Her eyelashes fluttered and her brows pinched again. She turned her face up to the sky. Kurt followed her gaze and felt cool flurries start to tickle his face.

"It's snowing," he remarked, in awe. "Does this mean we have to go back inside now?" He lowered his face back down to Mary's. Blinking through the heavy flakes, he was distracted just enough to almost miss the moment when Mary released his hand and laced hers around the back of her neck, bringing herself up to his face.

"Not yet," she said as she pulled him into her lips.

# Chapter 50

Mary knew that Kurt didn't want it to stop. Neither did she. But the snow was falling heavily now and their faces were wet and the cold was biting.

"Maybe we should go in now," she murmured as she rested back onto the heels of her snow boots.

Kurt took his hand and wiped the melted snow from her forehead and pulled her hood farther over her face. He muttered a protest, but let her tug him away.

"Come on," she let her hand slide down his jacket sleeve and fall into his. He let her lead the way.

They made it up onto the front deck within minutes. Mary stomped her boots on the wooden planks and then started to bend over to unzip them, when she felt Kurt behind her, pulling her up at the hips. In one, swift motion, he had wheeled her around- his back to the door with Mary facing him.

He raked his fingers under the back of her hair, tilted her face upward and stole another soft kiss. She let him, before pushing off him gently.

Kurt twisted the doorknob behind him and practically fell backward into the foyer. Mary stalled a moment, scanning the lodge for the others. When she saw none, she reached up and grabbed the back of his head, pressing her lips into his again.

The back door swung open and in sauntered Kato, Alex, and Rory, each yawning widely. Mary fell back in a flash, but Kurt kept his eyes on her.

"Oh, hey you two. Did we miss another team-building activity or something?" Kato joked. Mary couldn't tell if he could read them. Mary flushed a deep red.

Kurt pried his eyes from her and replied.

"Yes- snow angels. Out front. Have at it." He gestured to the front door. Mary made a quick mental note that snow angels and snowmen would be perfect for the next snowy retreat she put on. If she had the chance again.

The guys laughed and moved past Kurt and Mary and up the stairs.

"We're calling it a night. See you guys for breakfast," Alex responded as they ascended.

"Is Jace still outside?" Kurt asked after them.

"Naw, he went upstairs like five minutes ago. See ya."

Mary waited for them to shut themselves safely into their rooms before walking over to the dying fire and fixing her stare on the glowing embers.

Kurt joined her there asking, "Would you like me to add a log and get it going again?"

Mary turned to him. He took her chin in one hand and braced the other against her lower back.

She steadied herself against his chest and replied.

"We can let it die out. It's getting late."

Kurt frowned. "Not too late, I hope? It's our last night together."

Mary's face fell and she cocked her head. "It is?" Her breath caught in her chest. She sucked in the smoky air and pushed away from Kurt.

"No, no, no. That's not what I meant," Kurt backpedaled, but the damage was done.

Mary had to admit to herself that she was harboring trepidations about him all day. Was this whole weekend truly nothing more than a chance for him to "unwind?" What did he really think of her? Was she a small-town one-off to him? Had she misjudged his sincerity?

Mary glared at him; she couldn't help herself. She felt an insecurity rise up from her heart that she didn't know was there.

"What is this? What *is* this?" She demanded, flailing a hand between them and backing up so far that she nearly fell onto the hearth.

Kurt took a step toward her, ready to catch her. "That's *not* what I meant!" He raised his voice slightly, before remembering himself and checking the staircase behind him and the landing above. "That's not what I meant," he lowered his voice again and held his hands out, pleadingly.

"I thought I made it very clear that Anna and I are different. You may see her and how she acts in her personal life, but that isn't me." Mary felt her eyes well up and her lower lip tremble.

"I don't know what you're talking about. What does Anna have to do with this?" Confused, he dropped his voice again and begged, his eyes on fire.

"I like you, Mary. I want..." he imitated her gesture, waving his hands between them. "I want *this* to be *something*." At this, Mary froze.

"I'm not going to spend the night with you tonight, Kurt. If you thought that would happen, you're wrong," she started.

"I don't want that either," he cut in, desperate. But she held up her hand.

"I have gone back and forth all day about if you are the type of person I would even want to kiss, let alone fall for. I thought you were. But you just reminded me that *this* can't go anywhere. You live in the valley. You're going home tomorrow. You have a big life down there and too much to give up." She paused, catching her breath and finally unzipping her coat in order to shed it onto the love seat.

"But, Mary, if you're so willing to give up so easily, then did you ever really have any feelings for me?" It was Kurt's turn to feel slighted. Mary sank onto the love seat behind her, avoiding his eyes.

She crossed her arms over her chest and focused back on the red glow beyond the hearth.

Kurt joined her, easing himself onto the leather cushion.

Mary maintained her position and tried to ignore him. But he persisted.

"Mary," he continued, impatience filling his voice, "I meant everything I said. I am *so* into you. I will do whatever it takes to see you after this weekend. I'll drive up here every Friday. I'll call you ten times a day. When I said that it was our last night, I meant that I couldn't possibly go home without turning this into something more than a work event." He shook his head and fell back into the corner of the love seat. "That's what I meant."

Mary twisted around and looked at him. He seemed defeated. His hands covered his eyes and he let out a sigh. Mary had an urge to take his

159

bearded face in her hands and kiss him. Hard. But he interrupted her reverie and continued, leaning forward.

"I was married before," he gripped his knees with his hands and gave her an earnest look.

"I know. Anna had told me."

"It nearly broke me. I hated to get a divorce."

"Then why did you?" Mary cocked a skeptical eyebrow.

"I didn't want to. But," he sighed and clasped his hands in his lap. "I had no choice. She was long gone in the marriage. And, besides, she didn't want to have kids. I really, really did. It basically invalidated our entire relationship, in my eyes. And, I fell out of love with her anyway."

Mary felt he was holding more back, but she took in what he gave her. It was moving and it warmed her to hear that he was so serious about it all- marriage, children, the whole package. Maybe she had been presumptuous before.

"I'm really sorry to hear that," she replied honestly.

"You are?" He looked at her, somewhat unbelieving.

She smiled. "Yeah, I mean, well..." She searched the room for the right answer. "I'm sorry you had a bad time of it. But obviously, I'm glad you're..." She paused before finishing her sentence. "Single now?"

Kurt smiled back. "I was single when I came here."

# Chapter 51

Kurt pushed his sleeves up and Mary glanced down at his exposed forearms. He laced his fingers and flexed his hands out in front of himself in a stretch.

"Oh?" Her tone shifted, and she was flirting once again. He'd hoped beyond hope that he made his intentions crystal clear.

Mary shifted her weight, curling one ankle under her thigh and opening her shoulders to him.

He stared into her eyes, ready to make the move.

"I don't want to go home that way," he went on. He felt himself swallow the weight of his anxiety. He needed Mary to say yes. He needed her to agree.

He, simply, needed her.

"Did you suddenly forget that you're leaving in," she glanced at the clock that was sitting atop the mantle of the fireplace, "like twelve hours or so?"

"Now you understand my urgency." He wrapped his hands over her shoulders. "Let's take this further than just tonight."

Mary crumpled into him. He caught her, and they embraced, his face buried in the curve of her neck. She pushed back and their lips caught each other.

There was magic in the kiss.

As they parted, she read his mind.

"So, then, when *will* we see each other again? You guys are leaving early in the morning."

"Do you want to come to the valley? Maybe even next Saturday?"

"I have guests booked," her voice fell. Kurt thought about it for a minute. Then, he looked back at her and traced his finger around her face, hooking it under her chin, closing his eyes, and pulling her in to kiss her once more. When they opened their eyes again, he had an idea.

161

"The weekend after next is Christmas, right? I'll have a few extra days off. Maybe I'll just spend the holidays up here?"

Mary's eyes twinkled and a smile spread across her face.

"It can be a private retreat. We'll call it: *Christmas on Maplewood Mountain.*"

# Acknowledgments

I would like to thank a few special people for their support and help in writing, revising, editing, and formatting *Christmas on Maplewood Mountain*. Without them, I would be stuck at nothing more than a draft. Thank you to my advanced readers for their early feedback and positivity, especially Jeff Robinson. The same goes for my friends and family, who live far and wide. Your enthusiasm and love have sustained my efforts.

Of course, I never would have started without a muse or two. Thank you, Ed, for encouraging me to stick with it and offering important insight into the world of cryptocurrency and the mind of Kurt. Your own creative endeavors have always inspired me. And without you, I wouldn't have my reason: Little Eddie.

Finally, my mom and dad, who were my first fans. A special thanks, however, to my mom, who spent countless nights reading, re-reading, note-taking, and helping me turn a little idea into a finished book.